When The Music Gets Louder

Fidel Monte

BMN Publishing

Contents

Prologue

The bell that once called Mateo Aragon to prayer now echoed differently in his soul. No longer a summons to peace, it had become a reminder of the silence he carried, a silence heavier than the tolling of a thousand iron bells. Within the seminary walls, where holiness was meant to dwell, Mateo discovered shadows darker than any he had known in the world outside.

He had entered this sacred place seeking refuge—a sanctuary from the ghosts of his past, from the doubts that gnawed at him, and from the memories he had buried beneath layers of discipline and devotion. Yet, as the days unfolded, the sanctuary revealed itself to be another kind of crucible, one where trust could be weaponized and faith could be shattered.

The music of his vocation, once soft and distant, began to grow louder inside him, not as a hymn of peace but as a cry of anguish. Every note carried the weight of betrayal, of questions he dared not voice, of nights where silence suffocated more than any scream. And in that rising crescendo of torment, Mateo realized that he was no longer only running from the past—he was standing face-to-face with it.

Here, the pain he had attempted to flee from in Santa Ana and San Agustin had returned, assuming new shapes and clamoring for attention. The brokenness he had woven into resilience was tested again, this time by the very hands that were meant to guide him closer to God.

This is the story of how Mateo Aragon, scarred by betrayal yet strengthened by truth, learned that silence is not always holy and that sometimes the music of the soul must rise louder than the bells of the Church. It is a story of faith tried in flames, of wounds reopened, and of a man who refused to let the darkness define the final note of his song.

When the music gets louder, it can no longer be ignored.

CHAPTER I

Echoes of Silence

The bell tolled in the distance, its clear note cutting through the stillness of night. Mateo stood at the seminary gates with Diego at his side, the two of them breathing quietly in the cool air. Relief lingered in Mateo's chest, but so did a deeper weight—a knowledge that Diego's return was not the end of their struggles, only a fragile pause.

That night, Mateo prayed longer than usual, kneeling in the dim chapel long after the others had gone. His whispered petitions were not only for Diego but for all of them—Tomás, Emilio, and the brothers who had not yet found words for their own suffering. He prayed for strength, though he wondered if he even knew what strength meant anymore. Was it endurance? Was it silence? Or was it simply the willingness to stand beside one another in the dark, refusing to let go?

When he finally rose, his knees stiff, Mateo glanced at the crucifix above the altar. The candlelight flickered across the outstretched arms of Christ, and Mateo thought of his conversation with Emilio only days before. Perhaps this was the truest form of leadership—not guiding with certainty, but carrying doubt with dignity. Not solving, but staying.

The next morning dawned cool and sharp, the garden outside glittering with droplets from the night's rain. As Mateo entered the courtyard, he paused, inhaling the invigorating freshness that seemed to cleanse the earth itself. Yet within the seminary walls, the heaviness remained. At breakfast, muted voices and weary faces testified to burdens too heavy for their young shoulders.

Across the table, Tomás caught Mateo's eye and offered a small nod—silent encouragement, a reminder that he was not alone. Mateo returned the gesture, though in his heart he felt the storm clouds gathering again.

By midweek, the tension began to stretch thinner. Small irritations sparked into sharp words, and laughter, once so common among the brothers, became scarce. The seminary's rhythm of prayer and udy was steady, almost merciless, but it did little to quiet the restlessness that pressed in from every side.

In the common room one afternoon, it broke. Diego's frustration, carried silently for days, erupted with a force that startled them all. His outburst hung in the air, sharp and raw, and when he stormed out, silence filled the space he left behind. Mateo had tried to steady him with words, but even after Diego's return later that night, Mateo felt the fracture had not fully healed.

Now, in the days that followed, Mateo found himself unsettled. He bore his own doubts quietly, never speaking of them, but Diego's despair had given them a voice. Each time the bell rang, calling them to prayer, it echoed differently in Mateo's heart—less like comfort, more like command.

And there was something else. There was a small but insistent shift in how Father Alvarez's gaze lingered on Mateo during chapel. A pause, too long to be merely watchful. Mateo dismissed it at first—fatigue playing tricks on his mind, perhaps—but unease whispered at the edges of his thoughts.

He clung to his friendships, to the fragile bonds woven through shared pain. Emilio's quiet strength, Tomás's steady encouragement, even Diego's faltering steps forward—they gave Mateo purpose, an anchor against the tides of doubt. But in the silence of his own room, he felt it: the beginning of another trial, one that would not simply be weathered by brotherhood or prayer.

For even as the bells tolled with their measured certainty, a different music stirred inside him—louder, more insistent, and far more dangerous.

Mateo closed his eyes that night and whispered the same prayer he had spoken at the edge of despair so many times before:

Lord, do not let me fall. Not now. Not again.

But the silence that followed was heavier than any answer.

CHAPTER 2

The Gentle Snare

The rhythm of seminary life settled once more into its quiet routine. Prayer, study, and silence—the three pillars on which their days were built. Yet within the sameness, Mateo felt both restless and searching, as though something deeper called to him, just out of reach.

It was during one of those restless days that Father Alvarez drew nearer.

Among the priests, he was different. While others kept their distance, maintaining a formality that often felt cold, Fr. Alvarez carried an air of warmth. He spoke gently, never rushing, his words weaving both wisdom and comfort. In his presence, Mateo felt the ease of a son sitting before a father, unafraid of judgment.

"Mateo," Fr. Alvarez said one afternoon, after class had ended, "you carry silence differently from the others. It is not emptiness for you, but weight. Tell me, what burdens you?"

The question startled Mateo, not for its boldness but for the precision with which it pierced his heart. No one else had noticed—not Tomás, not Emilio, not even Diego in his fragile state. Only this priest.

And so Mateo spoke. Cautiously at first, then more freely, as Fr. Alvarez listened without interruption. He spoke of his doubts, his fears of failing as a leader, and his confusion about prayer that sometimes felt hollow. Fr. Alvarez nodded with a patience that seemed endless.

"You mistake weakness for failure," the priest told him softly. "But even Christ sweat blood in the garden. Do you think God loved Him less for that?"

Mateo lowered his gaze, words caught in his throat. The gentleness disarmed him. For the first time in weeks, he felt seen—not merely as another seminarian among many, but as Mateo.

Their conversations began to multiply. At first, brief exchanges in the courtyard or after chapel, but soon, longer moments in the quiet of the library or in Fr. Alvarez's small office. He had a way of turning guidance into friendship, of making Mateo feel as though their bond was unique.

On occasion, Fr. Alvarez would rest a hand on Mateo's shoulder as they spoke—a gesture so natural, so fatherly, that Mateo accepted it without question. Other times, the priest leaned close, lowering his voice, as though the wisdom shared between them was a secret entrusted only to him.

"You remind me of myself when I was young," he would say with a smile that carried both pride and intimacy. "So full of fire, yet uncertain where to pour it."

For Mateo, who had long carried doubts in silence, the closeness felt like grace itself. At last, someone understood. At last, someone saw him.

If there was any shadow behind the tenderness, Mateo did not notice. He saw only the refuge offered to him—a guiding hand in the dark, a voice of reassurance when his own faltered.

And slowly, without realizing it, he began to return more often to that voice.

One evening after compline, when most of the seminarians had retired to their dormitories, Fr. Alvarez beckoned Mateo with a quiet motion of his hand.

"Walk with me for a while," he said.

The seminary grounds at night were cloaked in silence, the only sound the soft hum of crickets beyond the walls. The two walked slowly under the dim lamps, their shadows stretching long across the cobbled path.

"Do you know why I asked you to walk with me?" Fr. Alvarez began.

Mateo shook his head.

"Because I see something in you that the others don't. You carry not only your own battles but also the wounds of others. You care too deeply to ever say it aloud. That is a rare gift."

Mateo's chest tightened. The words felt like both a comfort and a revelation. "Sometimes it feels like a burden," he admitted.

Fr. Alvarez stopped walking and turned toward him. "It will always feel that way until you learn how to pour it out." His eyes lingered on Mateo, steady and searching. "The soul, my son, cannot bear weight in solitude. It needs to be seen, to be unburdened, even in ways that words cannot always capture."

They resumed their walk, the priest speaking in a tone both tender and deliberate.

"Many young men come here thinking holiness is silence, distance, and discipline. And yes, discipline matters. But intimacy… intimacy with God, intimacy with a true guide… that is where the soul finds its strength."

The word lingered in Mateo's mind—*intimacy*. It felt almost out of place within the cold stone walls of the seminary, yet from Fr. Alvarez's lips, it sounded sacred, elevated beyond suspicion.

When they reached the steps of the chapel, the priest rested his hand lightly on Mateo's shoulder. "When you feel weary, or when prayer seems empty, come to me. Do not hold back. The deepest truths of the soul cannot always be spoken to many—they must be entrusted to the one who understands."

Mateo nodded, his heart swelling with gratitude. He had not realized until now how much he longed for such permission—to be vulnerable, to lay bare his fears without the weight of judgment.

"Good," Fr. Alvarez said, his voice warm, almost fatherly. "Then let us keep this bond between us. Sacred. Just you and me, as God intends for a true guide and his chosen disciple."

The words sank deep into Mateo's spirit. He did not see the hidden thread binding him tighter. To him, it was trust. To him, it was grace.

But in the stillness of the night, as the chapel doors closed behind them, Fr. Alvarez's hand lingered on his shoulder longer than necessary—gentle, almost imperceptible, but enough to sow the beginnings of a chain Mateo could not yet see.

CHAPTER 3

The Appointed Melody

The seminary breathed in rhythms that Mateo had begun to memorize—the rising bell at dawn, the ordered silence of morning prayer, and the voices rising in psalms as sunlight streamed through the chapel windows. Yet it was in music practice, every Monday afternoon, that Mateo felt most alive. The scattered chords of guitars, the uneven voices searching for harmony, and the shuffle of sheet music all seemed chaotic at first, but slowly, order would emerge from the disorder. For Mateo, it was like glimpsing the face of God through sound.

Fr. Alvarez, the seminary's music director, noticed this. He watched how naturally Mateo stepped in when others faltered, how his quiet suggestions encouraged the timid and steadied the unsure. There was something magnetic about the boy's way with music, a gift both instinctive and humble.

One evening, after practice ended and the choir filed out, Fr. Alvarez called Mateo aside. His hand rested on the young man's shoulder with reassuring weight.

"Mateo," he said, "you have a gift—not only for music, but also for guiding others. With my new parish assignment forty kilometers away, I cannot always be here. From now on, when I am away on Mondays, I want you to lead the choir rehearsals."

The honor felt immense. Mateo's chest tightened with a mixture of gratitude and nervous pride. "I'll do my best, Father," he replied earnestly.

The arrangement soon became routine. Each Monday, Mateo directed the practices, carefully guiding his peers through melodies and rhythms. Each week, when Fr. Alvarez returned from his parish duties, he asked Mateo for reports—listening closely to every detail, encouraging him, and affirming him. Their talks became a quiet bond of trust.

It was during one of these conversations that Fr. Alvarez leaned forward, lowering his voice as if sharing a secret.

"Mateo, you are a natural. But if you truly want to serve the Church through music, you must go beyond instinct. A true choir master must master piano and the language of music with all its symbols and signs. It is the foundation. Without it, your ability will remain… incomplete."

The suggestion startled Mateo. The seminary had no piano instructor, and though he admired the instrument from afar, he had resigned himself to never learning it. "But Father… where could I study?"

A knowing smile touched the priest's face. "My sister. She lives an hour's walk from here, and she has taught piano for many years. If you are willing, I can arrange for her to teach you every Saturday afternoon—for the entire year. It will require discipline, but by the end, you will not only play with skill but also understand the deeper structure of music. You will be prepared for greater responsibilities."

Mateo's heart leapt at the thought. Piano lessons! He pictured his hands finding melodies across the keys, learning to give voice to hymns in ways he had only dreamed. For a boy who often felt small and uncertain, the promise of such mastery was intoxicating.

"Would she really take me as her student?" he asked, almost in disbelief.

"Of course," Fr. Alvarez said, his tone warm but commanding. "I will speak to her myself. All you must do is commit. One year. Every Saturday afternoon. At the end of it, you will be a musician worthy of the calling I see in you."

The decision felt both heavy and thrilling. Mateo nodded with quiet resolve. "Yes, Father. I'll do it."

And so it was settled. Every Saturday, Mateo would leave the seminary after lunch, walking the long, dusty road toward the modest home of Fr. Alvarez's sister. For an entire year, those afternoons would be devoted to the piano—its keys, its theory, and its mysteries.

For Mateo, the piano appeared as a boon, a gateway to a realm he had long yearned for. He did not see the subtler threads being drawn tight around him—the way each note tied him more closely to Fr. Alvarez, binding him with gratitude, with dependence, and with trust.

For now, it was only music. Music and a mentor's guiding hand.

CHAPTER 4

The Long Walk to the Keys

The sun stood high above the seminary walls as Mateo stepped out through the gates, clutching a small notebook under his arm. The air was warm, the road dry and stretching endlessly before him. For the first time since arriving at the seminary, he was leaving its protective boundaries not for errands or parish duties, but for something personal—his very first piano lesson.

The walk was long, nearly an hour on foot. Dust clung to his sandals, and the cicadas shrilled from the trees. But each step only seemed to build his anticipation. He imagined himself sitting before a piano, pressing a key and hearing that deep, resonant voice answer back. For years he had listened to others play during liturgy or special celebrations, never daring to hope that he would one day learn it himself properly from an experienced piano teacher.

When at last he reached the small house of Fr. Alvarez's sister, he paused at the gate, wiping sweat from his brow. The house was modest, with flowers lining the walkway and a faint breeze carrying the scent of guava from a nearby tree. He knocked gently, and the door opened to reveal a woman in her late forties, wearing a plain dress, her eyes warm and inquisitive.

"You must be Mateo," she said kindly, her voice soft, as though she already knew him. "My brother has spoken of you. Please, come in."

The room smelled faintly of wood polish and sheet music. Against one wall stood the piano—black, slightly worn with age, but magnificent in Mateo's eyes. He felt a tremor of awe run through him, as if he were approaching an altar.

His new teacher smiled at the way he gazed at the instrument. "It's not as grand as the ones in the cathedral," she said, "but it will serve you well. Shall we begin?"

She showed him how to sit properly, how to rest his hands lightly on the keys, and how each note had its place in the great order of sound. At first, his fingers stumbled, striking wrong notes and uneven rhythms, but her patience steadied him. Slowly, he began to hear music take form—simple scales, then small melodies, each one like a door creaking open.

"You have good ears," she remarked. "That is a gift you cannot learn. The rest—discipline, technique, theory—we will build together, week by week."

By the time the lesson ended, Mateo's shoulders ached and his head swam with new knowledge. But his spirit soared. He thanked her with the sincerity of one receiving a rare treasure.

The walk back to the seminary felt shorter, though the sun was already sinking. Mateo carried with him not only the notes he had practiced but also the promise of an entire year of Saturdays—hours where he could escape into music, shaping his future one chord at a time.

That evening, Fr. Alvarez sought him out in the cloister. He listened patiently as Mateo poured out his excitement, recounting every detail of the lesson. The older priest smiled, his hand resting lightly on Mateo's shoulder.

"I'm glad you found joy in it," he said warmly. "Music will form you, Mateo. It will open doors you cannot yet imagine." He paused, his tone softening but firm. "But let me remind you—keep this opportunity between us. Not everyone will understand why you're receiving special lessons. Some might question it, or worse, envy it. If others ask, simply say you spent the afternoon in prayer and study. It is better that way—for you and for me."

Mateo hesitated for a moment. The secrecy felt unusual, almost unnecessary. But the trust he had in Fr. Alvarez outweighed his doubts. After all, hadn't this man already guided him, encouraged him, and believed in him when others barely noticed?

"Yes, Father," Mateo said, bowing his head. "I understand."

Fr. Alvarez smiled again, his eyes glinting with satisfaction. "Good boy. Now, rest well. Next week, you will go again. One year of lessons—one year of growth. I expect you to keep faithful to it."

As Mateo retired to his small cell that night, his heart still hummed with the echoes of the piano. He thought only of scales and chords, of melodies waiting to be learned. The caution of secrecy barely registered in his mind. What mattered most was that music, for the first time, felt like his own.

The weeks that followed unfolded with a rhythm all their own. Each Saturday afternoon, when the other seminarians rested or played football on the field, Mateo slipped quietly out of the seminary gates. He walked the familiar road—an hour there, an hour back—under sun, wind, and sometimes drizzle.

It became his secret pilgrimage, one no one else knew of but Fr. Alvarez.

At first, Mateo's fingers felt stiff and clumsy against the black and white keys. But with each lesson, his confidence grew. The piano no longer felt foreign; it began to breathe under his touch. The simple scales transformed into short hymns, then fuller pieces. His teacher's voice—gentle, precise, encouraging—guided him patiently, reminding him that mastery was not born overnight but shaped week after week, just as a stone is smoothed by the river's flow.

When Mateo played his first full hymn without error, his chest swelled with pride. He could almost hear the choir of angels joining him, every note carrying upward. "I can do this," he whispered to himself as he closed the fallboard of the piano, his hands still trembling from the joy of accomplishment.

On the long walk home, he often hummed the melodies he had just learned, letting them keep him company. He felt a freedom in those hours—alone with music, alone with dreams—that no sermon or lecture could provide.

Back at the seminary, he kept his lessons hidden, just as Fr. Alvarez instructed. When the others asked where he had been, he would lower his eyes modestly and say, "I spent the afternoon in study." It wasn't entirely a lie, he reasoned—music was a study, wasn't it? Still, a small unease sometimes stirred within him when he thought of hiding the truth. Yet, whenever he shared his progress with Fr. Alvarez, the unease melted away.

"You are learning quickly," the priest would say, nodding approvingly, his voice carrying a weight of authority that filled Mateo with reassurance. "One day, you will not just sing the songs—you will lead them. You will guide others in prayer through music. That is a gift few are given."

The praise filled Mateo with a warmth he had not known before. It was as though Fr. Alvarez saw something in him that no one else had ever noticed. He clung to that affirmation, measuring his worth by it, and in turn, he trusted the priest all the more.

But with every affirmation came the reminder: "Keep this between us."

Sometimes, when Mateo lay awake at night, he wondered why the affirmation had to be kept a secret. Wouldn't the seminary celebrate that one of their own was being trained so deeply in music? Wouldn't his classmates be proud? But then he recalled the stern but fatherly look in Fr. Alvarez's eyes and the way his voice softened into caution, and Mateo's doubts dissolved. Surely Father knew better.

Surely Father was protecting him from unnecessary envy or suspicion.

And so the pattern continued. Each week, Mateo walked the long road. Each week, his music grew stronger. And each week, so too did the quiet thread of secrecy that bound him ever closer to the priest who had given him this gift.

For Mateo, music was becoming more than just sound—it was his sanctuary, his language, and his promise of a future. Yet in the shadows of its melodies, unseen and unacknowledged, lay a trust so deep it would one day be tested.

By midyear, Mateo's playing had transformed from hesitant notes into flowing melodies. He could now accompany simple hymns, and he found joy in weaving his voice with the instrument—piano and singer becoming one. His teacher praised his diligence, telling him that not every student had the patience to walk two hours for a lesson each week. But Mateo did not mind. To him, the walk was part of his devotion, the cost of nurturing his gift.

The journey itself became a ritual. He memorized the bend in the road where wildflowers leaned toward the path, the crooked tree that seemed to bow as he passed, and the old wooden bridge that creaked like an old choir member struggling to stay in tune. Sometimes, as twilight colored the sky on his return, Mateo would close his eyes briefly and imagine the seminary walls echoing with the music he now carried in his heart.

Inside the seminary, no one questioned his absences anymore. They simply assumed Mateo preferred solitude or study, for he had always been quiet, never one to boast of himself. The secret settled on him like a second skin. At first, it had felt strange, like hiding a precious treasure. But gradually, it became normal, almost comforting, to know that this part of his life was known only to him and Father Alvarez.

It was their bond, unspoken yet deeply felt.

Whenever he reported back to the priest, Mateo would share what new scales he had mastered or what hymn he had learned. Fr. Alvarez always listened attentively, his gaze steady, his praise deliberate.

"You see, Mateo," the priest said one evening after choir practice, "discipline like yours is rare. Do you know why I ask you to keep this between us?"

Mateo hesitated, unsure if he should answer.

Fr. Alvarez leaned closer, lowering his voice, even though the chapel was nearly empty. "It is because not everyone understands how fragile a gift can be when it is young. People are quick to judge, to envy, and to diminish what they cannot comprehend. If they knew, they might interfere. They might rob you of this chance before you are ready."

Mateo nodded slowly. The words sank into him, wrapping themselves around his trust. He had never thought of it that way, but it made sense. If Father said it, it must be true.

That night, as Mateo walked back to the dormitory, he felt both proud and strangely burdened. The music was his joy, yes—but it was also a responsibility, one he must guard carefully. He promised himself he would never betray Father's trust.

And so, the weeks stretched into months. Each Saturday afternoon, Mateo's footsteps echoed on the long road to his lessons. His hands grew more fluent, his ear sharper, and his heart fuller. The piano was no longer simply an instrument—it was his confidant, his voice when words failed him.

But beneath the music, there grew something else, too: a quiet, invisible tether binding him more deeply to the man who had opened this hidden door.

CHAPTER 5

The Hand That Guides

The afternoon sun filtered gently through the wooden shutters, striping the keys in bands of light and shadow. Mateo's fingers hesitated on the piano, stumbling through a difficult passage that demanded agility he had not yet mastered. He pressed the piano keys carefully, his brow furrowed and his lips moving silently as if he were willing the music to obey him.

And then—unexpectedly—another hand rested lightly on his.

Mateo froze. The touch was firm but not forceful, confident yet gentle. He glanced sideways and saw Father Alvarez seated beside him, his calm face only a breath away.

"Relax," the priest said quietly, his tone smooth and reassuring. "You're tightening your wrist. That's why the notes sound uneven."

Before Mateo could respond, Father Alvarez adjusted his hand, guiding each finger to its proper place on the keys. Their hands moved together across the ivory surface, the priest demonstrating the natural curve of the fingers, the subtle shifting of weight that allowed music to flow without strain.

"Always remember," he explained, his voice low, almost like a secret, "the right fingering is not just about speed—it's about freedom. It allows the music to breathe, and you can move through it without effort. Try again, with me."

Mateo did as he was told. To his surprise, the passage sounded smoother and clearer. A rush of gratitude warmed him. "I see it now, Father. It's... easier."

Father Alvarez smiled, withdrawing his hand at last. "Good. You're learning quickly. Keep trusting the process."

The lesson continued, but Mateo found himself both focused on the notes and aware of the priest's presence beside him, like a silent force guiding him into deeper confidence. By the end of the hour, he felt exhilarated—he had unlocked something new in his playing.

When the lesson ended, Father Alvarez rose and stretched. "You've worked well today, Mateo. You have worked too well today to return to the seminary and sit alone until curfew. Come with me instead. I'm driving to my parish for an early dinner."

Mateo hesitated, surprised by the invitation.

As if anticipating the doubt, the priest added, "Don't worry. Today is Saturday—your brothers are all free until eight o'clock. No one will question where you are. Think of it as a small reward for your dedication."

The words dissolved whatever reluctance Mateo felt. He nodded, his face breaking into a smile. "Thank you, Father. I'd like that."

"Good," Alvarez replied, placing a hand briefly on his shoulder. "Then let's go. The road is long, but the food will be worth it."

Moments later, Mateo was seated beside him in the car, the countryside rolling past the window as the seminary receded behind them. For the first time in a long while, he felt as though he were stepping into a wider world—one filled with music, guidance, and the comforting certainty of Father Alvarez's approval.

The road stretched on like a ribbon of fading light, the seminary's stone walls long gone behind them. Mateo sat quietly, the faint hum of the engine blending with the echoes of the piano lesson still ringing in his head. His hands tingled faintly where Father Alvarez's had rested, not in discomfort but in the memory of guidance—firm, assuring, and strangely protective.

The drive ended in a small parish nestled at the edge of a quiet village. It was humbler than the grandeur of the seminary chapel—whitewashed walls, a modest bell tower, and a courtyard shaded by old acacia trees. Yet, it felt alive. Children darted through the yard, playing with sticks and balls, and an old man nodded respectfully as the car rolled past.

"This is where I spend most of my days now," Alvarez said as he parked. "It's new, still finding its soul. But with patience—and music—it will grow."

Inside the rectory, the air smelled faintly of wood polish and bread baking. A table was already set with steaming bowls of rice, a simple stew, and fresh mangoes sliced neatly on a plate. Alvarez gestured for Mateo to sit.

"Eat, hijo. You've earned it. Music demands energy, and you give it everything."

The words warmed Mateo. He hadn't been called *hijo*—son—by anyone since he left home. He smiled awkwardly and reached for the stew.

As they ate, Alvarez spoke with a quiet enthusiasm. He told stories of the parishioners—the widow who brought flowers every morning for the altar, the young couple preparing for their wedding, and the choir of children whose voices, he said, "could lift even the weary heart of God."

"Perhaps," he added with a knowing glance, "one day you will help me train them. They need someone young, someone who understands their hearts."

The thought startled Mateo. Him, leading a parish choir? He almost laughed, but Alvarez's eyes held his, steady and calm, until the idea didn't seem so far-fetched.

"I—I'd like that," Mateo admitted quietly.

Alvarez leaned back, satisfied. "Good. Then let's see where this path leads you. But remember, Mateo, not everyone needs to know the details of your journey. Growth happens best in silence."

Mateo nodded, not sensing any reason for suspicion. To him, the words sounded wise, even profound, the kind of advice a true mentor would give.

When the meal ended, Alvarez poured him a glass of sweet, warm ginger tea. The priest's voice lowered, almost intimate in its gentleness.

"Promise me one thing," he said. "That you will guard this gift—the music, your training, our work—like a secret garden. Only those who can nurture it should be allowed inside. Can you promise that?"

Mateo, his heart swelling with trust and gratitude, answered without hesitation.

"Yes, Father. I promise."

Outside, the parish bell chimed softly in the dusk. Inside, Mateo felt certain he had found more than a teacher. He had found someone who believed in him—someone who would shape him, guide him, and open doors to a future he could not yet see.

CHAPTER 6

The Circle of Trust

The weeks began to fall into rhythm, each one carrying the same secret cadence. Seminary life remained strict and predictable—morning prayers, study hours, chores, evening silence—but Mateo's Saturdays had become something more, something private and luminous.

Every Saturday afternoon, while the other seminarians busied themselves with rest, letters, or sports, Mateo slipped away toward the old road, where Father Alvarez would sometimes meet him or sometimes allow him to walk the familiar hour-long path to the house of Alvarez's sister. The piano lessons were steady, demanding, and often frustrating, but they carried the thrill of progress. Each week, Mateo's fingers grew more confident and more disciplined, guided by the patient hand of a teacher he was not supposed to know.

And each week, Alvarez's shadow hovered nearby—sometimes watching silently from a corner, sometimes stepping in with his own corrections, his hands settling lightly over Mateo's, steering them toward ease.

"Relax," Alvarez would whisper, his tone warm, almost paternal. "The hand must be free if the soul is to sing through the keys."

Mateo believed him. Why wouldn't he? Alvarez was not just the seminary's music director but also his personal guide—his mentor. No one else had ever invested in him this way. The secrecy no longer bothered him; if anything, it heightened the sense that he had been chosen.

When the lesson ended, there were often moments where Alvarez lingered with him, asking questions that felt weighty and personal: *How are you praying these days? Do you miss your family? Who do you trust most in the seminary?* Mateo, eager to please and be known, answered with honesty.

Alvarez listened as though no detail were trivial. He had a way of leaning forward, his eyes kind, his silence gentle, that made Mateo feel safe in offering pieces of himself.

The dinners at the parish became part of this rhythm, too. After certain lessons, Alvarez would invite him to ride along, reminding him of the Saturday free days and reminding him that no one would notice his absence. And each time, Mateo went willingly, drawn by the warmth of the rectory, the easy conversations, and the way Alvarez spoke to him, not as a boy but as a man with promise.

At the table, Alvarez would ask him to lead grace or to share thoughts from his scripture readings. Sometimes he would press a small book into Mateo's hands—a psalter, a volume of poetry, or a collection of sacred music—and tell him to keep it. *"This is between us,"* he would say, his tone more secretive than commanding. Mateo never questioned why.

In the parish garden, Alvarez taught him that music and holiness were inseparable. "Music is discipline, Mateo," he told him one evening, their steps crunching against gravel as fireflies sparked between the hedges. "And discipline is the key to holiness. What we build in secret, God rewards in the open. Remember that."

Mateo nodded, his chest swelling with pride. He did not see the calculation in Alvarez's eyes, only the admiration.

Back in the seminary, Alvarez would sometimes pause at his pew after night prayers, glancing Mateo's way with the faintest smile. Other times, passing Mateo in the corridor, he would murmur a quiet, "Courage, Mateo," as if to remind him of their hidden work.

By the middle of the year, Mateo could already sight-read simple hymns. The progress amazed him. But more than the music, it was the bond—the unspoken trust—that marked his days. He could not imagine refusing Alvarez anything.

And slowly, without ever realizing it, the circle of trust was closing around him.

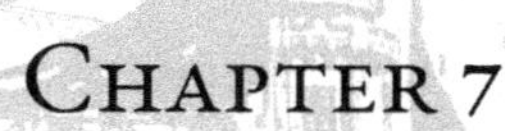

CHAPTER 7

The Extension of Time

It was a quiet Saturday in late October when the lessons began to feel different. The sun was softer now, slanting low through the windows of Alvarez's sister's sitting room, touching the worn piano keys with a pale glow. Mateo's fingers moved with a newfound confidence, weaving through scales and simple Bach preludes.

Alvarez was present again that day. At first, he stood behind the teacher's chair, observing in silence. But after a while, he leaned closer, offering small, precise corrections. His hand brushed Mateo's wrist lightly, repositioning it for smoother motion. His voice was calm, low, almost a murmur:

"Good, Mateo. Let the hand fall like water… Don't force it. Music is never forced—it is invited."

The lesson stretched longer than usual, spilling into the early evening. Alvarez's sister excused herself to prepare supper, leaving the two alone at the piano. Mateo barely noticed the passing of time; there was a sweetness in receiving guidance, correction, and affirmation.

When the lesson finally closed, Alvarez did not suggest their usual return to the seminary. Instead, he studied Mateo for a moment, his expression thoughtful.

"Mateo," he said softly, "I want to ask you something. You've been progressing quickly—faster than I expected. But to shape a true musician, sometimes an hour is not enough. There are moments when you need to linger… when you need space to grow without interruption."

Mateo looked at him, uncertain. "Do you mean… longer lessons, Father?"

"Exactly," Alvarez replied, smiling as if he were pleased with Mateo's intuition. "There are weekends when I finish at the parish early. Those evenings, I could bring you with me—to the rectory. Quiet time. We could study theory more deeply. You could practice at the parish piano, without distraction. Then I'll return you to the seminary before night prayers. No one would question it. After all, you are my assistant."

Mateo hesitated for only a moment before nodding. The idea felt almost like an honor, another step in the hidden apprenticeship that already filled him with pride. He trusted Alvarez completely—more than any teacher he had ever known.

"That would be wonderful, Father," Mateo said at last, his eyes bright. "I am keen to learn as much as I can."

Alvarez's hand rested briefly on his shoulder, warm and firm. "That's why I chose you, Mateo. Not everyone has the discipline. Not everyone has the gift."

The words burned gently into Mateo's chest, a mixture of humility and secret elation. He had been chosen. He belonged to something beyond the others, something private and precious.

That night, Mateo felt no doubt and no unease as he rode with Alvarez back toward the seminary, the road cloaked in silence and the hum of the engine. Only anticipation—of the music, of the learning, of the trust that seemed to grow stronger with every passing week.

He did not see that the lesson was no longer just about the piano.

CHAPTER 8

Lingering Hours

The first time Alvarez suggested Mateo remain longer at the parish, it sounded almost like an afterthought. They had spent the afternoon buried in sight-reading drills, with Alvarez walking him through hymnals and choral scores used for Sunday Masses.

"Notice," Alvarez had said, pointing at a page, "how the alto line sustains the harmony. Most people ignore it, but without it, the music collapses. You must train your ear to hear what others overlook."

Mateo nodded, eager, his pencil scratching notes in the margin of his notebook. He felt alive in those moments, as though Alvarez were revealing hidden codes that only true musicians could decipher.

By the time the sun dipped low beyond the parish windows, the lesson had stretched far beyond its usual frame. Alvarez closed the hymnal and leaned back, his face calm, almost weary.

"Mateo," he said gently, "it's later than I expected. The seminarians have already begun their supper. If I bring you back now, you'll walk into the refectory halfway through the meal, and everyone will look at you. It might draw questions."

Mateo blinked, startled. "I—I didn't notice the time."

Alvarez gave a small smile. "That's a good thing. It means you are immersed. But let us be wise. You may stay here and share a simple meal with me, and I'll return you to the seminary before the evening bell. Nobody will think twice."

There was something disarming in the way he said it—calm, practical, as if it were the most natural solution. Mateo experienced a brief surge of anxiety, but it swiftly gave way to a warm feeling of privilege. To be invited to eat at the parish, to be treated almost like an equal—it was more than he expected.

Dinner was modest: bread, soup, and a slice of cheese. Alvarez set the table himself, motioning for Mateo to sit. They ate quietly, the sound of spoons against bowls filling the air. Occasionally, Alvarez asked about his family, about his childhood in the province, and about the first song he remembered loving. Mateo found himself speaking more freely than usual, the priest's calm presence making it easy.

After the meal, Alvarez stood, stretched, and said, "Good. Now, let us return. The bell will sound soon."

The drive back was quiet, except for the soft hum of the radio playing a hymn. When they reached the seminary gates, Alvarez turned to Mateo, his voice low and firm.

"Remember, this arrangement is between us. It is not secrecy, but prudence. Others will not understand. They might envy or misunderstand my methods. But you, Mateo, must trust me. Do you?"

Mateo nodded without hesitation. "Of course, Father."

"Good." Alvarez smiled, placing his hand briefly on Mateo's arm before letting him step out into the night. "Then let us continue."

As Mateo walked back toward the dormitory, the chapel bells rang in the distance, calling the seminarians to evening prayers. He felt strangely lifted, as though he carried with him not just the music of the day but the quiet promise of something deeper—a bond others could not see, a hidden apprenticeship shaping him in ways he had yet to understand.

CHAPTER 9

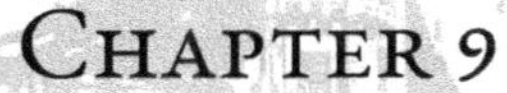

The New Rhythm

It happened again the following week.

At first, Mateo thought nothing of it. The Saturday lesson had once more stretched beyond the time he expected, his notebook filled with new exercises and his fingers stiff from practice. As the last notes of a hymn faded, Alvarez checked his watch and raised his brows.

"See? Past six already," he said casually. "If you return now, you'll miss the start of supper again. Better to wait."

The tone was light, almost dismissive, as though it were not a decision but simply the natural order of things. Mateo nodded, accepting without question when Alvarez suggested another meal at the parish.

By the third Saturday, it had become a pattern. The lesson, the realization of the hour, the invitation to stay for a meal—it was never planned, yet it always seemed to fall into place. Alvarez no longer explained it in detail; he only said, "We'll eat here," as though the matter were self-evident.

At first, Mateo told himself it was only temporary, a convenience until his schedule balanced better. But as the weeks went on, the new rhythm began to feel strangely secure. The parish kitchen grew familiar: the wooden table, the sound of cutlery, and the silence that followed their conversations.

He noticed that Alvarez asked fewer questions about music during those meals and more about *him*. He shared stories about his childhood in Sta. Ana and San Agustin, his favorite teachers, the games he played as a boy, and the lullabies his mother used to hum. Mateo often caught himself speaking more than he intended, surprised by how much he shared. Alvarez never interrupted, only listening, nodding, and sometimes smiling with a knowing look that made Mateo feel understood in ways no one else had managed.

After dinner, they would sometimes linger in the parish hall. Alvarez might open the piano lid again, guiding Mateo through scales in the dim light, his voice calm and low, the atmosphere softer than the sharp focus of the lessons earlier. Other times, they would simply sit in quiet, listening to the cicadas outside, as though silence itself were another kind of teaching.

By the fourth or fifth Saturday, Mateo realized that he no longer felt the need to rush back. Instead, he anticipated these evenings, when the parish seemed to close itself around him like a private world. Returning to the seminary after such hours felt almost like stepping out of a sanctuary into something less alive, less real.

Alvarez reinforced this thought gently, never forcefully. "You see, Mateo," he said once as they drove back under a sky heavy with stars, "true formation cannot always happen within the crowd. Sometimes God shapes us in hidden ways, in quiet places no one else sees. That is why you must guard this—our time—as something sacred. Understand?"

"Yes, Father," Mateo replied, his heart swelling with a mix of pride and humility.

He believed every word.

And so, without fully realizing it, Mateo allowed the quiet dinners and late drives to take root in his weekly life. What once felt like a rare privilege soon became routine, woven seamlessly into the fabric of his formation.

It was no longer unusual. It was simply the new rhythm of his calling.

Chapter 10

Gentle Corrections

The parish room where Mateo practiced the piano began to feel like an extension of himself. Each Saturday, the same faint smell of polished wood, the filtered light through the tall windows, and the quiet solitude before Alvarez arrived. It was no longer just a lesson—it was a place where Mateo felt seen.

That afternoon, Alvarez leaned closer as Mateo stumbled through a hymn, his fingers faltering over a difficult passage.

"No, no," Alvarez said gently, placing his hand over Mateo's. "You're reaching too stiffly. Let your wrist loosen." His fingers pressed softly against Mateo's knuckles, guiding the hand downward, then upward in a slow arc.

Mateo nodded, grateful for the correction. Alvarez didn't withdraw immediately; instead, he lingered just long enough to demonstrate the motion again, his voice steady and reassuring.

"You mustn't fight the music," he explained. "It should feel as though the notes are flowing *through* you, not forced out of you."

There was nothing harsh in his tone. In fact, there was kindness, even warmth—an encouragement Mateo rarely experienced among the strict discipline of seminary life.

Over the following weeks, these gestures became part of the lessons. A hand on his shoulder to adjust his posture. A gentle press on his back to remind him to breathe deeply. Fingers resting lightly over his own to show the correct spread across the keys.

Each touch was purposeful and practical, and Mateo never questioned it. In his view, this was simply the way great teachers trained their students. He remembered his elementary school teachers tapping his wrists with a pencil to keep them from collapsing at the piano—this was no different, only gentler and more personal.

Occasionally, when Alvarez corrected him, he would offer a quiet laugh, as though they shared a secret. "There, you see? Already smoother." Or, "Now it feels right, doesn't it?" Mateo would nod eagerly, a warmth rising in his chest at the praise.

One evening after a lesson, Alvarez closed the piano and rested his hand briefly on Mateo's shoulder. "You've grown so quickly," he said softly. "Not just in skill, but in spirit. God is clearly shaping something rare in you, Mateo."

The words lingered with him long after he returned to the seminary. Rare. Special. Chosen.

No one had ever spoken to him like that before.

And so, Mateo leaned into every correction, every word, and every gesture, unaware of how carefully Alvarez was blurring the lines between guidance and something else. To Mateo, it was still mentorship—an intimate, holy kind of care that only deepened his trust in the priest, who seemed to see him more clearly than anyone else ever had.

Chapter II
An Invitation to Stay

The parish grew busier as the months passed. Fr. Alvarez's new assignment demanded more of his weekends, and there were times when he arrived late for Mateo's lessons, his face drawn from long hours of travel and pastoral work.

One such Saturday, the sky had darkened quickly with the threat of rain. The clouds hung low and heavy as Mateo played scales at the upright piano, the sound nearly drowned by the drumming of raindrops on the tin roof.

Alvarez arrived halfway through the lesson, shaking the water from his coat. "You'll be soaked through if you walk back to the seminary tonight," he said, glancing at the storm outside.

Mateo shrugged. "It's not the first time I've walked in the rain, Father. I don't mind."

Alvarez smiled faintly and placed a hand on the boy's shoulder. "Still, it isn't wise. You could fall ill—and besides, I'd rather not think of you trudging an hour back in the dark." He paused, as though weighing his words carefully. "Why don't you stay here tonight? The rectory has a spare room. In the morning, I'll drive you back before prayers. No one will even notice."

Mateo hesitated. Staying overnight felt unusual, but Alvarez's tone was casual, almost fatherly. The offer made sense; the storm was worsening, and the walk home would indeed be miserable.

"Are you sure it's alright?" Mateo asked.

"Of course," Alvarez replied warmly. "You're like a son to me. I wouldn't leave my own son walking out in weather like this."

That word—*son*—settled deeply into Mateo's heart. Being regarded with such affection and closeness was rare in his life. He felt something like pride swell in him, a reassurance that he truly mattered.

Dinner was simple: bread, cheese, and a pot of stew that Alvarez warmed on the stove. They ate in the rectory's kitchen, the rain pelting the windows, the little room filled with the faint smell of herbs and smoke. Alvarez asked about Mateo's classes, his family back home, and his hopes for the future.

It felt less like a priest speaking to a seminarian and more like a father listening to his son.

Afterward, Alvarez showed him to the spare room. The bed was small but clean, with folded sheets that smelled faintly of lavender.

"Rest well, Mateo," Alvarez said, pausing at the door. "Tomorrow, we'll continue your lessons before I drive you back. Think of this as your home, too. You're safe here."

Mateo lay awake for some time, listening to the storm fade into the night. Safe. The word wrapped around him like the blanket across his shoulders. He believed it, fully, completely.

The priest had given him not only music but also shelter, care, and trust. And in his innocence, Mateo did not see the careful, deliberate weaving of threads—threads that bound him closer and closer to a man whose intentions were far from what they seemed.

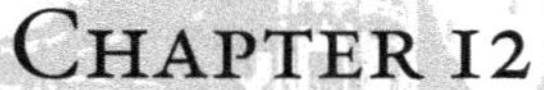

CHAPTER 12
The Morning After

The church bells from the small parish woke Mateo at dawn. Their ringing carried softly through the walls of the rectory, blending with the smell of coffee drifting from the kitchen. He stretched beneath the unfamiliar sheets, momentarily forgetting where he was until the memory of the storm and Alvarez's invitation returned.

For a brief moment, guilt pricked him—he had not slept in the seminary, had not joined the others for night prayers. But then he remembered Alvarez's words: *Consider this to be your home, too. You're safe here.* The reassurance settled him.

When Mateo entered the kitchen, Alvarez was already there, cassock loosely draped over his shoulders, sleeves rolled up as he poured coffee. He looked less like a priest at that moment and more like a father beginning the day in his own household.

"Sleep well?" Alvarez asked.

"Yes, Father. Very well." Mateo took the seat offered at the table.

"Good," Alvarez said, placing a cup before him. "You'll need your strength today. Before we drive back, I want you to sit at the piano again. I find mornings are the best time to play—the hands are rested, and the mind is clearer."

The lesson was different that day. Alvarez stayed close, listening intently to Mateo's scales, correcting fingering with gentle touches, and sometimes guiding his wrists with both hands.

"You see," Alvarez explained, his voice low and patient, "music flows when the body learns to relax. If you tense up, even the simplest passage will sound forced. Let the hand fall naturally—like this." He placed his hand over Mateo's once again, pressing lightly. "Do you feel it? How does the weight carry the sound?"

Mateo nodded eagerly, repeating the movement. The priest's nearness no longer startled him; it seemed natural, part of the learning process. Alvarez never hurried, never raised his voice, and he was always calm and affirming.

When the lesson ended, Alvarez offered him breakfast—a warm plate of eggs and bread. They ate together in companionable silence, the air filled with the ticking of the rectory clock.

As Mateo gathered his things, Alvarez leaned against the doorway, regarding him with a quiet smile.

"You played beautifully today. You're growing quickly—not just in skill, but in discipline. That pleases me." His tone softened. "I don't often say this, but I trust you, Mateo. I know you'll honor this path."

Mateo felt a flush of pride. In the seminary, trust was crucial, and receiving such special attention brought him a quiet joy.

On the drive back, Alvarez spoke of the future. "One day, when I'm away, you'll direct the choir and teach others, too. Imagine that—you, passing on the very skills you're learning now. But remember, Mateo..." He glanced at him, his voice lowering. "These lessons are just between us. Others may not understand. They might think I'm giving you special favors. And we wouldn't want that, would we?"

Mateo shook his head, quick to agree. "No, Father."

The car hummed along the road. Mateo looked out the window at the countryside flashing by, unaware that with every secret kept, every private word, the bond between him and Alvarez was being tied tighter, drawn deeper into silence.

CHAPTER 13

A Secret Between Two

When Mateo returned to the seminary that Sunday afternoon, nothing seemed out of place. The courtyard buzzed with the usual noise of seminarians returning from their free day: some laughing over stories from the town, others lingering in quiet corners, rosaries in hand. The bell for Vespers rang, and everyone fell into line as though nothing had shifted.

Yet for Mateo, something had.

As he knelt in the chapel that evening, the words of the psalms drifted over him, but his mind was elsewhere—back in the rectory, at the piano, with Alvarez's voice guiding him. The memory of the priest's praise still warmed him, louder than the chant of his fellow seminarians.

He told himself it was nothing unusual. After all, Alvarez was his mentor, his guide, and his teacher. But even as he repeated the words silently, a subtle awareness pressed in: no one else knew about his lessons. No one else knew about the trip to the parish. The thought made him both uneasy and strangely proud, as though he carried a treasure too delicate for others to touch.

The week unfolded in its familiar rhythm: morning prayers, classes, and study hours. Mateo moved through them as always, but he noticed how easily his attention wandered to Monday afternoons. The choir practice, once an ordinary duty, now felt like a privilege, a continuation of Alvarez's trust in him. The seminarians followed his lead, never suspecting how much of his newfound confidence came from those quiet mornings in the parish rectory.

One afternoon, as they left the chapel, Mateo's friend Carlo nudged him playfully.

"You've been different lately," Carlo said. "More… serious. Almost as if you're hiding something."

Mateo laughed, masking his surprise. "Hiding? What could I possibly hide here? You know everything about me."

Carlo grinned, unconvinced, but let the matter drop. Still, the words lingered. Mateo realized for the first time that keeping secrets required practice. He had to train his expressions, his voice, and even his laughter so no one would ever guess.

By the following Saturday, anticipation thrummed in him. He waited until the appointed hour, heart racing as he slipped quietly away from the seminary grounds. He knew the path well now—the hour-long walk to Alvarez's sister's house, where the piano lessons began. And though fatigue sometimes weighed on him, each step felt purposeful, as though he was walking not only toward music but also toward a destiny Alvarez himself was shaping for him.

And always, at the back of his mind, Alvarez's caution echoed: *"These lessons are just between us. Others may not understand."*

Mateo had accepted the rule of silence without hesitation. What he did not yet see was how deeply that silence was already binding him—not only to music, but to the man who had made himself its gatekeeper.

CHAPTER 14

The Presence That Stayed

The first time Alvarez appeared during Mateo's lesson, it had seemed like a coincidence, almost a gift. Mateo had welcomed the surprise and even enjoyed the gentle corrections that gave his playing new life.

But it didn't stop there.

Two Saturdays later, as Mateo settled onto the worn bench of the upright piano, he caught sight of a figure at the door. Fr. Alvarez entered without announcement, as though it were the most natural thing in the world. He greeted his sister, then took a seat nearby, his hands folded as he watched.

At first, Mateo felt nervous under the priest's gaze. His fingers stumbled on scales he had practiced a dozen times. But Alvarez smiled patiently, offering small gestures of encouragement—*steady your wrist, relax your shoulders, let the melody sing*. The tension melted, replaced by a quiet pride in knowing Alvarez thought it worthwhile to be there.

In the weeks that followed, Alvarez's presence became less occasional and more expected. Sometimes he would arrive midway, sometimes from the very start. Each time he found a reason—checking on his sister, ensuring Mateo's progress, or simply "passing by."

The priest never interrupted harshly. His corrections were always subtle, gentle, and wrapped in the language of mentorship. He would lean over, guiding Mateo's fingers with his own, demonstrating a phrase until the notes flowed seamlessly. Mateo accepted the contact as part of learning, grateful for the attention.

One Saturday, when Alvarez placed his hand lightly on Mateo's shoulder as he played, Mateo barely flinched. The gesture, once surprising, had become familiar, almost reassuring.

After lessons, Alvarez often walked Mateo part of the way back toward the seminary. Their conversations wandered—about music, faith, and even the responsibilities of priesthood. To Mateo, these walks felt like glimpses into the life he longed for, a life of service and knowledge, carried forward by someone he trusted.

Still, Alvarez never failed to remind him:

"These lessons are for you, Mateo. For your future. Not everyone would understand the effort we're making together. Best to keep it quiet."

Mateo nodded each time, his loyalty deepening with every step. The secrecy no longer felt like a burden but a sign of their closeness—an invisible thread binding him to Alvarez, beyond the eyes of his peers.

And so, what began as piano lessons with a stranger's sister slowly transformed into something else: a world where Alvarez was no longer simply a visitor but a constant presence, woven into every chord Mateo played.

CHAPTER 15

The Road That Beckoned

The first trip to the parish with Alvarez had felt like a reward, a small adventure Mateo never expected. The car ride had been filled with laughter and stories, and the meal afterward had tasted richer than anything served at the seminary. Mateo had gone to bed that night with a sense of gratitude—perhaps even pride—that Alvarez had chosen him.

Weeks passed, and one Saturday, as the lesson ended, Alvarez casually asked, "Would you like to come along again, Mateo? I'll be heading to the parish tonight."

Mateo's heart lifted. He nodded eagerly.

And just like that, a new rhythm formed.

Almost every other Saturday, Alvarez would extend the same invitation, always framed as an afterthought, as though Mateo's company was not expected but simply welcome. Sometimes they drove in silence, the hum of the road filling the space. Other times, Alvarez spoke about parish life—the challenges of starting a community from nothing, the joy of hearing a congregation grow in song.

Mateo listened intently, soaking in every word. To him, these trips felt like stepping into the future, like standing on the edge of the calling he was preparing for. Alvarez spoke as though he were confiding in a peer, not merely a student. That trust thrilled Mateo.

Dinner at the parish house was always simple: bread, soup, or rice with fish. Yet Alvarez served it with the warmth of family, pulling Mateo into conversations that made him feel less like a seminarian and more like a brother. Sometimes they lingered after eating, talking in the dim glow of the rectory, Alvarez asking about Mateo's dreams, his childhood, and his fears.

But always, before they returned, came the reminder:

"You know, Mateo, it's best if this is just between us. The seminary has rules... and sometimes people misunderstand what they don't see."

Mateo agreed every time, without hesitation. He understood. Alvarez wasn't asking him to lie—just to protect something precious.

And so, the routine quietly took root. Lessons on Saturday afternoons. A drive in the countryside. An evening of music, food, and quiet companionship. They returned before the gates closed, ensuring that no one was aware of their presence.

What began as a rare gift became a pattern, a thread that wove its way into Mateo's weeks until he could no longer imagine Saturday without Alvarez's shadow beside it.

The parish road, once unfamiliar, now felt like a path he was meant to walk—each step binding him closer to the man he trusted most.

CHAPTER 16

The Gentle Hand

The evenings at the parish had become familiar, almost comforting. Mateo looked forward to them, counting the days until Saturday would arrive again. To him, they were not just excursions—they were escape. Escape from the rigid bells of the seminary, from the endless rules, and from the watchful eyes of formators. In Alvarez's parish, he was not simply one seminarian among dozens; he was *chosen*. Seen. Trusted.

The routine was often simple. A quiet drive out of town, a meal prepared in the rectory kitchen, and occasionally, a long walk in the parish garden. Alvarez spoke to Mateo as no other priest had ever done before—not with distance or cold authority, but with warmth, laughter, and something Mateo could only describe as *friendship*.

One particular evening, the two sat on a wooden bench beneath the stars. The garden smelled faintly of damp earth and wild grass. Mateo was recounting a story from his boyhood choir, his hands gesturing in the air as he mimicked the old choirmaster's scolding voice.

Alvarez laughed, his deep chuckle carrying through the night. "And yet, from that scolding, came the voice I hear now," he said, his hand finding Mateo's shoulder. The touch was light, almost fatherly, but it lingered just long enough for Mateo to notice. "You've carried music in your bones since you were a boy. God must have been smiling the day He gave you that gift."

Mateo felt warmth rise in his chest. Compliments from Alvarez always felt heavier, more meaningful than from anyone else. To him, praise seemed like truth.

Another time, after a late supper at the rectory, Alvarez insisted on driving Mateo back to the seminary. The roads were quiet, the headlights carving paths through the dark. As the car slowed near the seminary gates, Alvarez reached across the seat, ruffling Mateo's hair with a grin.

"You've done well today, hijo," he said softly, the

Spanish word—*son*—ringing in Mateo's ears long after he stepped out of the car.

That word. It held Mateo like an embrace. He had not been called "son" in such a tender way since he could remember. It left him carrying an unfamiliar ache, part longing, part joy.

At the piano lessons, too, Alvarez's presence began to be felt more tangibly. Initially, he would merely listen in silence as Mateo's fingers stumbled over the scales. But soon, he would rise from his chair, step behind Mateo, and gently press a hand between his shoulder blades.

"Sit straighter," he would murmur. "Breathe from here; let the music flow."

At other moments, Alvarez's palm would rest lightly on Mateo's wrist to ease the tension. "Your hand must float, like this," he explained, guiding the fingers across the keys. His touch was deliberate, always framed in the language of music, always cloaked in the authority of teaching.

And to Mateo, there was nothing strange about it. If anything, it made him feel cared for. It made him believe he was worth the effort of a mentor who was willing to correct him not only with words but also with patient guidance.

If Alvarez's hand lingered a second longer than necessary, Mateo did not notice. If Alvarez's praise came wrapped with a gaze that held him a heartbeat too long, Mateo only felt gratitude. Gratitude that someone as respected as Father Alvarez had chosen him, out of all the seminarians, to mold and shape, both musically and spiritually.

The web was delicate, invisible to Mateo, spun thread by thread. A guiding hand on the keys. A palm steadying his wrist. A ruffle of the hair after a car ride. A word—*hijo*—spoken in just the right moment to soften his defenses.

None of it raised suspicion. On the contrary, it deepened trust.

Mateo walked back into the seminary each time with a quiet smile, convinced he had found not only a teacher but also a true father in faith, a man who saw him for who he was and who he could become.

He did not know, could not know, that the line between mentor and disciple was already blurring, almost imperceptibly, with each passing week. What he believed to be guidance and affection was slowly becoming something else—something that, for now, felt safe.

Safe. Intimate. Even holy.

And Mateo welcomed it all without question.

CHAPTER 17

The Chosen One

Saturday afternoons had become the rhythm of Mateo's year. No matter how grueling the week, he lived for the moment the bell tolled, releasing the seminarians into their free day. For most, it meant letters home, long naps, games of basketball, or even outings. For Mateo, it meant the piano. It meant Alvarez.

This Saturday was no different—at least, not at first. The lesson began as usual; Mateo bent over the keys, working through a Clementi sonatina, his fingers stumbling over the cross-hand passages. Alvarez corrected him with quiet patience, his hand once more guiding Mateo's across the black-and-white keys.

But when the music was set aside, Alvarez did not dismiss him. Instead, he leaned back in the chair beside the piano, watching Mateo with a seriousness that unsettled him.

"You know," Alvarez began slowly, "I do not let anyone else in the seminary know of our arrangement."

Mateo blinked, unsure how to answer.

Alvarez's voice softened. "It is not because I am ashamed. No. It is because I see something in you that I do not see in the others. A gift. A hunger. A soul that listens—not just with ears, but with the heart."

The words washed over Mateo like a blessing. His chest tightened, a mix of pride and disbelief. To be singled out by Alvarez was no small thing.

Alvarez continued, "That is why I guard this. Why I keep it between us. Others would not understand. They would only be jealous… or suspicious. But you, hijo—you are different."

The Spanish word again, *son*. Mateo swallowed hard, his eyes cast down to the keyboard. "I… I don't know what to say, Father."

"Say nothing," Alvarez replied gently, his hand resting on Mateo's forearm. "Only know that I trust you. And that you must trust me."

Mateo nodded. The touch was steady, not forceful, but it carried weight. It felt like a pact sealed in silence.

Later that evening, Alvarez invited him once more to the parish rectory for dinner. Mateo hesitated at first—there was always the unspoken risk of being noticed—but Alvarez dismissed the concern with a wave. "No one will question where you are. Saturday is your day. And besides," he added with a faint smile, "you are safe with me."

The meal was simple, but Alvarez's presence made it feel like a feast. Over roasted chicken and rice, he spoke to Mateo not as a priest to a seminarian, but as a confidant. He asked about his fears, his dreams, and his frustrations. And Mateo, caught in the warmth of that rare attention, answered with more honesty than he had ever given anyone.

As the evening drew on, Alvarez poured two small glasses of wine. He raised his glass lightly. "To you, Mateo," he said, his eyes holding the boy's. "To your music, and to what you will become."

Mateo, flushed with surprise, lifted his own glass. He had never toasted before—not like this. In that moment, he felt older, elevated, as though he had been allowed into a circle that no other seminarian even knew existed.

As the night drew to a close, Alvarez disappeared briefly into his study. Mateo sat waiting, still warmed by the glow of wine and words, when Alvarez returned carrying a book—its cover worn, its edges frayed from years of use.

He placed it gently on the table before Mateo.

"This," Alvarez said, his voice low, "was given to me when I was your age, by my own mentor. It has followed me through conservatories, through choir lofts, and through every parish I have served. It is more than a book—it is a companion."

Mateo's eyes widened. The book was thick, bound in faded leather, with the title stamped in gold: *The Great Classical Masters*. Inside, Mateo could see scores from Mozart, Beethoven, and Chopin—pieces he had only ever heard whispered about in theory class, never touched with his own hands.

"I want you to have it," Alvarez said.

Mateo looked up, startled. "Father, I—this must be very important to you. I can't—"

Alvarez silenced him with a raised hand. "It is important, yes. Which is why I give it to you. You will honor it. You will live it. Music like this—" he tapped the book, "—requires more than fingers. It requires devotion. A soul willing to carry it. And you, Mateo, have that soul."

The words settled on him like a mantle, heavy and yet exhilarating. He reached out and touched the book as if it were sacred.

Alvarez leaned closer, his eyes steady. "But this, too, must remain between us. Others would not understand. They would see it as favoritism. They would say it is unfair. They do not see what I see. You are set apart."

Mateo's throat tightened. He felt both humbled and lifted, chosen in a way he could not put into words. "I'll take care of it, Father. I promise."

Alvarez smiled faintly, almost like a secret shared. "I know you will."

The ride back to the seminary that night was quiet. Mateo kept the book clutched in his lap, his fingers tracing the cover over and over. It felt heavier than any textbook he had ever carried, heavier because of what it meant—not just music, but trust, destiny, and belonging.

He slipped into the dormitory unnoticed, placed the book carefully under his pillow, and lay awake long after the others had fallen asleep.

The phrase repeated in his mind, in rhythm with the ticking clock: *Set apart. Set apart. Set apart.*

CHAPTER 18

The Secret Rehearsal

The seminary's music room was quiet on most afternoons, except on Mondays when the music practice was going on. It was here, in a forgotten corner by the tall windows, that Mateo found his sanctuary. The heavy book Alvarez had given him remained hidden under his mattress most days, but when the chance arose—on free hours, or when others were distracted—he would slip it into his satchel and disappear into the music room's silence.

Opening the pages, Mateo felt as though he were entering another world. The notes—Mozart's intricate dances, Chopin's sighs, Beethoven's storms—were unlike anything in the seminary's modest music books. They were vast landscapes, and he was a pilgrim stepping cautiously into them.

At first, he stumbled. Fingers tangled, rhythms faltered. But Alvarez's voice echoed in his mind: *"Don't be afraid of mistakes. Let the music correct you."* Slowly, with patient persistence, the phrases began to shape themselves under his hands.

The piano in the music room was old and slightly out of tune, but to Mateo it felt alive. He pressed into the keys with reverence, as if each sound unlocked something hidden within him. Sometimes, the music was so beautiful it startled him—he would stop playing, his breath caught, afraid he had awakened something he could not yet understand.

He noticed, too, how his secrecy added to the intensity. Each stolen hour felt like a sacred ritual, a devotion offered in silence. No one knew—no one could know. Alvarez had made that clear.

One evening, after choir practice, Alvarez approached him quietly. "You've been reading the book?"

Mateo nodded, shy but proud. "Yes, Father. I—Beethoven's *Moonlight Sonata*. It feels… like it's speaking."

Alvarez's eyes narrowed, almost glowing. "Ah. Then you are ready."

"Ready for what?" Mateo asked.

Alvarez placed a hand on his shoulder. "For discipline. For beauty that demands sacrifice. These pieces are not for everyone. Only those willing to give themselves fully." His grip tightened slightly. "You are such a one, Mateo. That is why I chose you."

The words sent a warmth through Mateo's chest, mingled with a flicker of unease. Chosen. The word had returned, heavier this time, almost binding.

That Saturday, Alvarez was waiting by the seminary gate. Instead of their usual route to his parish, he led Mateo to the small chapel in the parish grounds—a place dim, candlelit, and echoing with quiet. On the piano by the altar, Alvarez placed the book.

"Play," he said simply.

Mateo hesitated, then opened the pages to Beethoven. The music rose in the candlelight, fragile yet luminous, wrapping itself around the chapel walls. Alvarez stood close, listening, occasionally leaning over to guide a hand, to correct a fingering, or to whisper encouragement.

When the final chord faded, Alvarez looked at him with a mixture of pride and intensity. "You must guard this gift. Guard it as you would your soul. Do you understand?"

Mateo nodded, though something in him trembled.

That night, as he returned to the seminary, the weight of the book under his arm felt heavier than ever. Not just a gift, not just music—something deeper, binding, secret, demanding.

And yet, despite the faint unease that stirred in his chest, Mateo longed for the next Saturday to come.

Chapter 19

The Discipline of Obedience

Saturday afternoons became the rhythm of Mateo's hidden life. Each week, he slipped out quietly, the heavy book tucked under his arm, heart racing with anticipation. The lessons were no longer just about scales or fingering—they had become something larger, a weaving of discipline, silence, and loyalty.

In the small parish chapel, Alvarez was always waiting. Sometimes he greeted Mateo with warmth, other times with silence so austere it made the young seminarian nervous. The music books were spread on the piano, pages ready, candles flickering in the quiet air.

"Before you play," Alvarez would say, "you must still yourself. The music cannot live in a restless heart."

He made Mateo sit in silence for long stretches, hands folded, eyes closed, listening to the stillness. At first Mateo fidgeted, but over time he began to understand: the pauses, the quiet, and the waiting were part of the discipline. The music flowed differently after the silence, as though his fingers carried something deeper than mere notes.

One day, as Mateo prepared to play, Alvarez placed a hand firmly on his shoulder.

"Remember," he said softly, "obedience is the first step to mastery. The great composers you love—Mozart, Chopin, and Beethoven—each was obedient. To rhythm. To structure. To the laws of music. Without obedience, their genius would be chaos."

Mateo nodded. "Yes, Father."

Alvarez's voice lowered. "So it is with us. The discipline you learn here, with me, is not for anyone else to see. It is not for the others in the seminary. They would not understand. Do you see why this must remain between us?"

Mateo swallowed, feeling again the weight of secrecy pressing against his chest. "Yes, Father. I won't tell anyone."

A smile flickered across Alvarez's face. "Good. Then you are ready for more."

He opened the book to a new piece—Chopin's *Nocturne in E-flat Major*. The notes flowed like liquid silver, but Alvarez stopped him often, guiding his hands, leaning close, and correcting finger by finger.

"Not like that, Mateo. Relax the wrist. Yes, feel it. Let the sound breathe. There—do you feel the difference?"

Mateo nodded, his cheeks warm, his body tense under the priest's presence. And yet, he marveled at how the music suddenly sounded fuller, more alive.

Afterwards, Alvarez leaned back, his eyes intent. "You see? Music obeys only when the player himself has learned obedience. If you give yourself fully, it will answer you wholeheartedly. But you must not doubt. You must not question."

Mateo felt the words settle in him like a vow. Music. Obedience. Silence. They had become one and the same.

That night, returning to the seminary late, Mateo lay awake in his narrow bed. His roommates slept soundly, their breaths steady in the dark. But Mateo's mind was alive, replaying every word, every gesture of Alvarez, and every sound from the piano.

The secret weighed on him. And yet, he did not resent it. On the contrary—he cherished it. To be chosen, to be trusted, to be shaped in silence… it felt like carrying a treasure only he and Alvarez understood.

For the first time, Mateo thought: *Perhaps this is what it means to have a vocation—not only to God, but to something greater than myself.*

CHAPTER 20

The Quiet Tests

It began with small things.

One Saturday, as Mateo prepared to return to the seminary, Alvarez said, almost casually, "Stay a little longer. The chapel needs to be locked, and I must leave early. I'll trust you with the keys. Return them to me tomorrow."

Mateo hesitated. To stay longer meant arriving late for evening prayers, a breach of seminary discipline. His heart raced. But Alvarez's eyes were steady, almost commanding.

"Yes, Father," Mateo whispered.

When he returned late that night, slipping into the dormitory, no one stirred. Relief washed over him.

It was only a small thing, but it marked the first time Mateo chose Alvarez's word over the seminary's rule.

The following week, another test came.

Alvarez placed a new sheet of music before him—Schubert's *Ave Maria*.

"This one is for you," he said, his voice quiet but deliberate. "Learn it well. But do not play it in the seminary chapel, not even for practice. Do you understand?"

"Why not, Father?" Mateo asked timidly.

"Because this piece is not for them," Alvarez replied, eyes narrowing. "It is for us. Between us. Some treasures lose their meaning when shared carelessly. You must learn to guard what is precious."

Mateo lowered his gaze. "Yes, Father."

And so, *Ave Maria* became their secret song. Mateo practiced it only in Alvarez's parish, the melody sinking into his fingers like a prayer whispered in the dark. Each note carried both beauty and weight, as though the music itself knew it was forbidden elsewhere.

But the greatest test came on a rainy Saturday in late October.

The storm raged outside, wind howling against the chapel windows. Mateo had lingered after his lesson, waiting for the downpour to ease. Alvarez stood by the door, cloak in hand.

"You'll not be going back tonight," Alvarez said. "The roads are flooded; the walk is impossible. You'll stay here."

Mateo's chest tightened. "But the seminary—"

"I will take responsibility," Alvarez interrupted firmly. "Your absence will raise no questions. Remember, this is why I warned you: not everyone must know. Do you trust me, Mateo?"

The words hung in the air, heavy and decisive.

Mateo felt a shiver run down his spine. He thought of the seminary rules, the prefects, and the strict schedules—all of which would be broken if he stayed. And yet, Alvarez's presence, steady and commanding, drew him in.

"Yes, Father," he said finally. "I trust you."

That night, Mateo lay on a small cot in the parish rectory, the storm still raging outside. He could not sleep. Not because of the rain, but because of the unease in his chest—the realization that he had crossed another line, one he could not easily return from.

But when morning came, and Alvarez praised him for his obedience, the unease dissolved into a strange warmth. To be tested and to be found faithful—it filled Mateo with a pride he had never felt before.

In the weeks that followed, he found himself awaiting the next test, the next moment Alvarez would draw him deeper into silence and trust.

For Mateo, obedience had become more than discipline. It had become belonging.

Chapter 21

Unspoken Gestures

The weeks following the storm passed quietly, but something in Mateo's lessons had changed. Mateo felt it most when Alvarez stood beside him at the piano. Before, the priest's guidance had been firm and distant: pointing at notes, correcting rhythms, or tapping the desk in time. Now, his presence felt closer, almost tangible.

When Mateo's fingers fumbled on a passage of Mozart's *Sonata in C*, Alvarez leaned in. His hand did not seize Mateo's but rested lightly on his wrist, guiding the flow of his movement.

"Not so stiff," Alvarez whispered. "Feel the phrase breathe. Music must live in your hands."

Mateo nodded, his pulse quickening, though he could not say why.

Other moments followed. A hand on his shoulder when he found the right chord. A gentle pat on his back after finishing a piece. Even a light touch on his hair once, with a quiet, almost fatherly smile.

To anyone else, these gestures might have seemed like nothing. But to Mateo, whose life in the seminary was ruled by distance and discipline, each small act felt heavy, carrying more warmth than he had known for years.

Still, Alvarez never let him forget the rules of secrecy.

One afternoon, as Mateo gathered his books after practice, Alvarez said, "Remember, our work depends on trust. Do not speak of your lessons. Not to your friends, not even to the rector. This… connection we share is not for everyone to understand."

Mateo swallowed and nodded. "I understand, Father."

"Good," Alvarez said, his gaze steady. "Some gifts must be protected, lest they be misunderstood and broken."

Mateo carried those words with him. At night, lying in his seminary bunk, he thought of them over and over. He told himself that the secrecy was proof of his value—that Alvarez trusted him with something sacred, something worth guarding.

But sometimes, late in the chapel during silent prayer, another thought whispered in his mind: *Why me?* Out of all the seminarians, why had Alvarez chosen him?

The question lingered without answer, and yet it filled Mateo with a quiet pride. To be chosen meant he was special. And for now, that was enough.

Chapter 22

Beyond the Notes

Saturday afternoons were no longer just for piano lessons. Over time, Alvarez began to weave other requests into their meetings. At first, they were small, almost incidental.

"Mateo, could you carry this folder to the sacristy? I forgot to leave it with the altar servers."

Or, "Would you mind helping me arrange the hymnals in the parish before we return to the seminary?"

Mateo never hesitated. Each task felt like a privilege, a proof of trust. To serve Alvarez beyond the piano made him feel as if he were stepping into a wider world—a world just beyond the borders of the seminary, alive with parishioners, families, and the hum of ordinary life.

One Saturday, Alvarez handed Mateo a sealed envelope.

"Take this to the parish treasurer," he said quietly. "Tell her it's the monthly report. Don't give it to anyone else, and don't mention that you carried it."

Mateo did as he was told. He walked the short path from the rectory to the small parish office, his heart swelling with a strange pride. He was no longer just a student; he was a trusted aide, a companion in responsibility.

Afterward, Alvarez treated him to an early dinner in the parish hall. The two of them ate simply—bread, soup, and a little cheese—but to Mateo it tasted rich, better than anything the seminary had offered all week. Alvarez spoke not as a distant priest but as someone almost fatherly, asking about Mateo's family, his memories of childhood, and his secret dreams for the future.

It was during those dinners that Mateo began to notice the rhythm of Alvarez's influence. Music in the afternoons. Parish tasks in the evenings. Private conversations afterward, filled with words that lingered in Mateo's heart long after he returned to the seminary.

Yet, always, there was a reminder of silence. "You must not speak of these errands," Alvarez told him one night as they locked up the parish. "The seminary has its rules. They would not understand. What we build together is delicate—it must be kept safe."

Mateo nodded, eager to prove his loyalty. He felt chosen, set apart from his peers, drawn into a bond that seemed both secret and sacred.

And in that secrecy, Alvarez's presence grew heavier in his life—no longer just his teacher of music but the keeper of doors Mateo had never imagined opening.

CHAPTER 23
The Night of Shadows

The parish house was unusually warm that evening, filled with the aromas of roasted meat and freshly baked bread. Alvarez had gone to lengths to prepare a "special dinner" for Mateo, speaking cheerfully as though the table had been set for a feast. Mateo, flattered by the gesture, allowed himself to relax. He had grown used to these private moments—moments when Alvarez's company seemed to lift him above the ordinary world of seminary routine.

When Alvarez poured the wine, Mateo hesitated. Drinking was not part of their usual dinners. But the priest insisted with a smile, saying, "A celebration of progress. You've earned this." Reluctantly, Mateo lifted the glass.

The first sip was sharp, unusual, but the warmth of the food made it easier. By the second glass, however, something shifted. His body felt heavy, as though a thick curtain had fallen over his limbs. His eyelids drooped uncontrollably. He tried to sit up straight, tried to keep the conversation alive, but every movement grew sluggish, like wading through water.

"You're tired," Alvarez observed, almost soothingly. "There's a room prepared for you. Rest tonight. Tomorrow, we'll return refreshed."

Mateo nodded weakly. He remembered being guided down the narrow hall into the small guest room. The bed was neatly arranged, the blankets tucked with care. He tried to say something—perhaps a word of thanks—but the weight of exhaustion silenced him. Within moments, the world went black.

What happened in the hours that followed would never form a complete picture in Mateo's mind. Fragments would surface later: a pressure he could not push away, a hand that lingered too long, a fleeting moment of struggle smothered by his own body's betrayal. Yet none of it remained sharp enough to grasp. It was as though his memory had been wrapped in fog, leaving behind only an unshakable sense of violation.

When morning came, Mateo awoke slowly, his body strangely sore, his mind hazy. The sunlight streaming through the window felt cruel in its brightness. He lay still, staring at the ceiling, trying to gather the threads of the night before. Something had happened—something he could not name, but felt in his bones.

Alvarez greeted him at breakfast with his usual calmness, speaking of Mass preparations and parish duties as if nothing were amiss. Mateo, still dazed, could only nod and follow. Yet beneath the surface, an unease had taken root. He knew, without being able to articulate it, that a boundary had been crossed.

It was the beginning of a silence that would cost him more than he could yet imagine.

CHAPTER 24

The Silence Between

The week that followed blurred into a haze of routine. Mateo went to morning prayers, attended classes, and fulfilled his chores—yet everything felt muted, as though the world had lost its sharpness. The bell that once rang with clarity now echoed in his chest like a hollow drum.

Every so often, an image would flash unbidden: the darkened room, the weight of exhaustion, a sensation he could not name pressing against his will. Then nothing—just a suffocating blankness. He shook his head, convinced he was imagining it, but the unease in his body betrayed him.

At meals, he found himself eating less. During recreation, his laughter seemed forced and brittle. He avoided the other seminarians' eyes, as though they might see through him to the storm he could not voice.

On Saturday, when he returned to Alvarez for another lesson, his chest tightened. Would the priest mention it? Would he acknowledge the strange fog of that night? But Alvarez was as composed as ever. He greeted Mateo warmly, corrected his fingering at the piano, and spoke about Bach as though nothing had happened.

At dinner, Alvarez leaned forward and said softly, "You must be careful not to exhaust yourself, Mateo. The mind plays tricks when the body is weak. Rest is important." His tone was kind, but there was a weight in the words—a subtle suggestion that what Mateo remembered was nothing more than a dream.

Mateo nodded, though his stomach knotted. He wanted to ask, to confront, but his tongue felt heavy. The very thought of speaking filled him with a dread he could not explain. If he was mistaken, if it truly had been a dream, what shame would he bring upon himself by suggesting otherwise?

That night, back in the seminary, Mateo lay awake staring into the dark. For the first time since entering, he felt utterly alone. He wanted to pray, but the words caught in his throat. His loyalty to Alvarez, the man who had opened doors to music and encouragement, now sat uneasily beside a new and unspoken fear.

Silence became his refuge—and his prison.

CHAPTER 25

The Price of Perfection

Nearly a year had passed since the first time Mateo laid his fingers on the ivory keys. What began as hesitant, uneven sounds had grown into flowing passages of Mozart, Beethoven, and Chopin. The discipline he once struggled to impose on himself for seminary life had been transposed into music, his hands driven by the same relentless energy that fueled his prayers and duties.

Every afternoon, he practiced until his knuckles ached and his back stiffened. Four hours a day became his norm, the rhythm of scales and arpeggios woven into his life like the tolling of the chapel bells. His evenings were filled with theory exercises, chord progressions, and harmonic analysis. He consumed the language of music as though it were scripture, memorizing and internalizing it with a devotion that astonished even his teachers.

By now, Mateo was preparing for his final performance piece—a composition so demanding that only the most advanced students dared to attempt it. Fr. Alvarez had chosen it for him, insisting that Mateo had not only the technical skill but also the artistry to carry it through. *"With this piece,"* Alvarez said one afternoon as he watched him play, *"you will stand among the finest. You will not only qualify for the highest piano grade—you will prove that discipline and faith can sculpt greatness."*

Mateo's heart swelled with gratitude for those words. Without Alvarez, none of this would have been possible. He had provided him with access to music, to guidance, to a future that Mateo had never imagined. For this, he was profoundly thankful.

And yet, each night when the lights dimmed and the quiet of the dormitory wrapped around him, a different struggle returned. The unexplainable fog of that one night at the parish house—the memory he could never fully grasp, yet could never completely forget—lingered like a shadow over his spirit. It gnawed at him as he lay in bed, heavy with exhaustion. Sometimes it came as a fleeting sensation, a brush of unease against his skin. Other times, it struck as a sharp pang in his chest, leaving him restless until dawn.

He tried to pray it away. He tried to bury it beneath the notes of his piano pieces, drowning his confusion in endless practice. But silence always crept back. In the silence, he faced the questions he dared not ask.

By day, Mateo was a rising musician, admired for his skill and dedication. By night, he was a boy haunted by something unnamed, torn between gratitude and suspicion, between admiration and fear.

And as the date of his final performance drew near, he realized that he was not only preparing to prove himself musically—he was struggling to find the strength to face what his heart could no longer ignore.

CHAPTER 26

The Performance

The sun rose golden that morning, washing the seminary walls in light that seemed to demand excellence from everyone who walked its halls. For Mateo, it was more than a morning—it was a threshold. Nearly a year of relentless practice, late-night drills, and whispered prayers had brought him here: the final piano examination.

His classmates did not know. To them, he was only quieter than usual, perhaps lost in thought. Only Fr. Alvarez knew what this day meant. He had arranged everything—the private audition room, the examiners, the score, and even the heavy silence that seemed to press around Mateo as he entered the hall.

The grand piano waited in the center like an altar. Its polished black surface reflected Mateo's nervous face as he approached. He sat, breathing carefully, trying to steady his hands.

The first notes began softly, almost fragile, like a voice testing its courage. But soon, the music surged—cascading runs, strong chords, and passages that demanded both precision and abandon. Mateo's fingers moved with a discipline born of sacrifice, every movement recalling hours of repetition. Each phrase carried not just sound but the weight of his life inside the seminary: obedience, loneliness, gratitude, and confusion.

Halfway through, his hands faltered. Just for a breath. His chest tightened with a memory—Alvarez's approving smile, the wine glass that had left him dizzy, the shadow that followed him into sleep. A tremor of doubt shook him.

But then, almost instinctively, Mateo lifted his eyes for a moment and whispered in his heart, *"Let the music carry me."*

And it did.

His hands steadied. His body yielded to the instrument, no longer forcing but flowing. The piano became his confession, each note a cry of both devotion and hidden anguish. The arpeggios rose like prayers, the sustained chords lingered like unspoken fears, and in the thunder of the final passage, Mateo found a strength that startled even himself.

When the last note faded, there was silence. A silence so deep that Mateo felt it inside his bones. Then, quietly, one of the examiners nodded, as if recognizing not just the technique but the truth behind the performance.

Fr. Alvarez, seated at the back, clapped softly, his eyes gleaming with pride. Mateo lowered his head, torn between gratitude and unease, feeling as though he had bared his soul on that instrument more than he had ever done in words.

He had passed the test with flying colors—but the battle within him had only just begun.

CHAPTER 27

The Afterglow

The applause still echoed faintly in Mateo's ears as he rose from the piano bench. His legs trembled, partly from exhaustion and partly from the adrenaline that still surged through him. He had given everything he had to the performance, leaving nothing hidden, nothing restrained.

The examiners spoke in low voices, their pens scratching across paper, and then one of them leaned forward with a rare smile.

"You have a gift," the man said. "Not just in technique, but in spirit. It is rare to see someone so young command the piano like this."

Mateo bowed his head, unable to find words. His throat was tight with a strange mixture of pride and unease. He should have felt free, light, and victorious. But instead, a weight pressed against his chest—as though the music had opened a door inside him that he could not close.

Fr. Alvarez was waiting outside the hall. As soon as Mateo stepped into the corridor, the priest's hands gripped his shoulders firmly. His smile was radiant. "Magnificent," he whispered, his voice filled with warmth. "I have never been more proud of you."

The words should have been a comfort, but they sank into Mateo's heart like a stone. Still, he managed to smile, because gratitude demanded it. Gratitude—and loyalty. Without Alvarez, there would have been no piano lessons, no chance at this level of mastery, and no moment like today.

"Thank you, Father," Mateo said softly.

Alvarez pulled him into a brief embrace, holding him just long enough for Mateo to feel both protected and cornered. Then, with a hand on Mateo's back, the priest guided him toward the car waiting outside.

"Tonight, we celebrate," Alvarez said. "You have earned it. There are no obligations at the seminary, no bells, no duties. Just you, me, and the joy of your triumph."

Mateo hesitated for the briefest moment, but the memory of the performance filled him again. He wanted to believe in Alvarez's words. He wanted to hold onto the pride of the day without letting fear stain it.

As the car pulled away, Mateo gazed out at the fading sunlight, his hands folded loosely in his lap. He told himself he deserved this—a night of rest, of honor, of being seen not as just another seminarian but as someone who had accomplished something remarkable.

And yet, in the stillness of his own heart, he could not silence the small, insistent whisper: *At what cost?*

CHAPTER 28

The Celebration Dinner

The restaurant glowed with golden light as the evening crowd filled its tables. Chandeliers hung from the ceiling like clusters of captured stars, scattering warmth over polished wood and crisp linen. The hum of voices, the clink of cutlery, and the faint notes of a violin drifting from a small ensemble near the corner all blended into a gentle music of their own.

Fr. Alvarez held the door open for Mateo, who entered hesitantly. He had never been in such a place before. The seminary refectory was plain, orderly, and utilitarian—food was nourishment, not an occasion. Here, however, everything spoke of indulgence: rich aromas of roasted meats and buttered sauces, servers gliding between tables with trays like dancers, couples and families leaning close, their faces lit with laughter.

Mateo felt out of place. He looked down at his hands, still bearing faint marks of practice—calluses near the fingertips, a small bruise on the side of his thumb where he had pressed too firmly against an octave. He thought about hiding them under the tablecloth, ashamed that his body revealed how much he had labored for this day.

Alvarez noticed his unease and leaned in, his voice calm, reassuring.
"Lift your head, Mateo. Tonight is yours. You've earned every bit of this."

They were led to a quiet table near the far wall, away from the busiest part of the dining floor. Mateo sat opposite Alvarez, trying to steady himself.

The menu was overwhelming, filled with dishes whose names he had never heard before. Alvarez ordered without hesitation—roasted lamb with rosemary, a bottle of deep red wine, and a selection of appetizers. Mateo said nothing, trusting his mentor to guide him even in this unfamiliar space.

As the bread and cheese arrived, Alvarez raised his glass.
"To you, Mateo," he said. "To your discipline, your brilliance, and the future that is waiting for you. Few

men your age would endure the hours you have. Fewer still could have played as you did today."

Mateo flushed, his ears burning. He lifted his glass of water, clinking it softly against Alvarez's. "Thank you, Father. I… I could not have done it without you."

The words were true. Yet as soon as he spoke them, something stirred uneasily in him. Gratitude was natural, but dependence—that was something deeper, heavier. He tried to shake the thought, focusing instead on the meal before him.

The lamb was tender, the flavors unlike anything he had tasted before. Each bite seemed to dissolve on his tongue, rich and intoxicating. Alvarez watched him with a quiet satisfaction, as though Mateo himself were the feast.

"Do you realize," Alvarez said, resting his elbows on the table, "what doors will open for you now? With your grade level, you could pursue the conservatory, perhaps even beyond our country's borders. Music could become your language to the world."

Mateo's heart leapt at the thought. He had never allowed himself to dream that far. A conservatory? Beyond the country? It sounded like another life altogether. He saw himself on concert stages, saw audiences rise to their feet, and saw music carrying him far from the narrow walls of the seminary.

But then, just as quickly, the vision faltered. The seminary. His vows. His calling. And Father Alvarez. Would leaving mean betraying the very man who had made this dream possible?

"I don't know if I am ready for all of that," Mateo admitted, lowering his eyes.

"You are ready because I have made you ready," Alvarez said firmly. His tone was still warm, but beneath it lay a weight of ownership. "Every note you played today bore my guidance. Remember that, Mateo. Never forget where your strength comes from."

The words landed in Mateo's chest with a thud. He smiled faintly, because that was the only response he could give. But deep inside, he felt the threads tightening—invisible cords binding him to Alvarez's hand. Yes, gratitude, but also something more binding— something harder to name.

The wine arrived then. Alvarez poured generously into his own glass, then into Mateo's. The liquid shimmered in the light, dark as velvet.

"Just one sip," Alvarez urged. "A night like this deserves it. You are not a child anymore, Mateo."

Hesitating, Mateo lifted the glass. The wine was heavier than water, carrying a warmth down his throat and into his chest. It made him flush and made his body feel looser. Alvarez smiled at the sight, content.

As the evening deepened, their table filled with empty plates and half-finished dishes. Mateo's head swam, partly from exhaustion, partly from the wine that Alvarez refilled without asking. His body was tired, but his heart was conflicted—caught between joy and unease, between triumph and a growing shadow he could not define.

When the bill was paid and the restaurant began to quiet, Alvarez leaned close across the table. His voice was soft, almost tender.

"Come back with me tonight, Mateo. You deserve to rest in comfort. Tomorrow will come soon enough, but this evening—this victory—it is ours."

Mateo hesitated. A small, trembling voice inside urged caution. But his body was weary, and his spirit, still basking in the glow of the day's success, longed for rest. Alvarez's eyes held his, steady and unyielding, and Mateo found himself nodding.

Outside, the night air was cool, with stars scattered faintly across the dark sky. Mateo followed Alvarez to the waiting car. The celebration had filled him with pride, yet underneath it all, he carried the faintest sense of surrender—the recognition that each step forward bound him closer to the man beside him.

And in the silence of the ride, he could not shake the question: *Whose dream was he really living now?*

CHAPTER 29

The Quiet House

The drive back from the restaurant was silent. The only sound was the low hum of the engine and the occasional shift of gravel beneath the tires. Mateo leaned against the window, his body heavy from the meal, his head still light from the wine. He tried to keep his eyes open, but the darkness of the night, combined with the warmth in his veins, pulled him toward sleep.

Alvarez, meanwhile, drove with calm precision. His hands rested lightly on the wheel, but his posture was straight and composed. Every so often, he glanced at Mateo—a quiet smile flickering at the corners of his lips.

When they arrived, Alvarez's house stood waiting, its windows glowing faintly against the night. It was a modest building by some standards, but to Mateo it seemed large, even grand, compared to the seminary dormitory. The front door opened with a soft click, and they stepped inside.

The air was warm, carrying the faint scent of incense and polished wood. Alvarez placed a hand on Mateo's shoulder, guiding him toward the sitting room.

"Sit down for a while," he said softly. "You need not rush to sleep."

Mateo obeyed, sinking into a chair. The cushions gave way beneath him, and for the first time in months, he felt what true comfort could be. The walls around him were lined with books, framed photographs, and religious icons. But interspersed with the sacred were signs of another life: paintings of landscapes, a crystal decanter with amber liquid, and a piano in the corner with its lid lifted slightly, as though waiting for touch.

Alvarez poured himself a small drink and, after a pause, poured one for Mateo as well. He handed the glass over.

"Only a sip," he said again. "It will help you rest."

Mateo took it reluctantly, letting the liquid brush against his lips. The taste was sharp, burning at first, then fading into warmth. He set the glass down quickly, unwilling to take more.

Alvarez sat across from him, studying him as though he were a painting, every line of his face holding some secret worth uncovering.

"You played beautifully today," he said, his voice low. "Do you realize how rare your gift is? Most men could practice a lifetime and never touch what you touched."

Mateo shifted uncomfortably. Praise still unsettled him, especially when spoken so intensely. "It is the Lord's gift," he murmured.

Alvarez leaned forward. "Yes. But the Lord chooses instruments. And He chose you. And He gave me the privilege to shape you."

The words settled heavily. Gratitude, again, but also a reminder—a claim. Mateo nodded, not trusting himself to answer.

The clock on the mantle ticked softly. The room felt both intimate and vast, filled with shadows that seemed to lean closer. Alvarez stood suddenly.

"You are tired," he said. "Come. You will sleep in the guest room tonight. You deserve better than the hard seminary bed after such a day."

Mateo rose, his legs unsteady. Alvarez led him down a quiet hallway. The guest room was simple but inviting: a wide bed dressed in clean sheets, a lamp casting a soft glow, and a small desk at the corner.

"Rest here," Alvarez said, setting a hand briefly at Mateo's back before stepping aside. "Tomorrow, the world can wait. Tonight, let peace be yours."

Mateo slipped off his shoes and sat at the edge of the bed. His eyelids drooped, heavy with fatigue. Alvarez lingered a moment in the doorway, watching.

"You should be proud," he said gently. "Do not let doubt steal from you what you have earned."

Mateo nodded faintly, laying down against the pillow. His body surrendered almost at once, though his mind still flickered with fragments—the restaurant, the applause in the hall, Alvarez's voice telling him he was chosen.

As his consciousness drifted, he felt—or thought he felt—a hand brush against his hair, smoothing it back from his forehead. The touch was tender, almost fatherly, yet it carried a weight that unsettled him even in his half-dreaming state.

He wanted to open his eyes, to speak, but sleep pressed too heavily upon him. He slipped under, into darkness, the echo of Alvarez's presence lingering in the room like incense after Mass.

And in his dreams, triumph and unease blended together, leaving Mateo caught in a silence that felt both sacred and dangerous.

CHAPTER 30

The Morning After

The light came slowly, spilling into the room through the half-open curtains. It was the kind of soft dawn that usually brought Mateo peace at the seminary: birdsong, pale sky, the promise of another day of prayer and work. But here, in Alvarez's guest room, that same light felt strange, almost intrusive.

Mateo stirred beneath the sheets. His body was heavy, as if he had run for hours the day before, though he knew he had only played piano, eaten, and spoken with Alvarez. His head ached dully. Even lifting his arm felt sluggish, his joints resistant to movement.

He lay still for a moment, eyes closed, trying to recall the night. He remembered the restaurant clearly—the meal, the quiet drive back, Alvarez's smile as they sat in the library. He remembered the second glass of wine, though he thought he had only sipped it. After that, the memories blurred, breaking apart like fragments of a dream.

Something had happened. He could feel it in his bones, though he could not name it. It was as if his body remembered more than his mind, and that thought alone unsettled him.

With effort, he sat up. The sheet slipped from his shoulder, and for a brief instant he caught the faintest scent on the fabric—incense mixed with something else, something musky, unfamiliar. He frowned, pulling the sheet closer to himself as though to shield against a truth he could not yet face.

The door creaked. Mateo turned quickly.

Alvarez stood in the doorway, already dressed in his clerical black, his face calm, composed, as though he had been awake for hours. He carried a tray with a cup of coffee, steam rising gently, and a plate of bread.

"Good morning," Alvarez said softly, his voice warm. "I thought it best to let you sleep. You needed it."

Mateo forced a smile, though his throat felt dry. "Good morning, Father."

Alvarez set the tray down on the desk. "The recital took much from you. Even a strong body like yours has limits. Drink—it will steady you."

Mateo nodded, reaching for the cup. The coffee was strong, bitter, and it jolted his senses awake. Still, the fog in his mind lingered. He wanted to ask, "*what happened?*" but the words stuck. To ask was to accuse, and he had no proof, only shadows of memory.

Instead, he said, "I… I feel so tired still. As if I did not truly rest."

Alvarez's gaze held his for a long moment before softening. "It is nothing unusual. When the spirit is tested as yours was yesterday, the body suffers. Do not be troubled. This house is a place of rest."

Mateo lowered his eyes, unsure. He wanted to believe him. After all, Alvarez had guided him through music, through discipline, through faith itself. But beneath the surface, something twisted—a whisper that told him not everything was as it seemed.

They ate in silence, broken only by the clink of cup against saucer. After a while, Alvarez said, "Your performance is nearly ready for the final evaluation. I see in you not only talent but also endurance. A year ago, you would never have imagined sitting here, preparing for the highest level."

"Yes," Mateo murmured. "It is… a blessing."

Alvarez leaned forward slightly. "More than a blessing, Mateo. A calling. And you must trust me when I say that your path will not be easy. You will be misunderstood. You will be envied. Even by those closest to you. That is why loyalty matters. Trust matters. Without it, your gift could be destroyed."

The words pressed against Mateo like a weight. He nodded, though unease gnawed at him. His loyalty to Alvarez was already deep—but last night had planted a seed of doubt, a crack that no amount of praise could seal completely.

When Alvarez left the room, Mateo sat motionless, staring at the half-empty cup of coffee. He tried again to piece together the night: the weight of sleep, the brush of a hand on his hair, the scent in the sheets. His heart quickened. He shook his head, refusing to let suspicion take full shape.

And yet, when he closed his eyes, he felt it again—that sense of something having crossed a line while he was too weak to resist.

For the first time since he had entered Alvarez's mentorship, Mateo whispered a prayer not of gratitude, but of confusion:

"Lord… what is happening to me?"

CHAPTER 31

In the Stillness of the Chapel

The chapel had always been Mateo's refuge, but recently it had become more than that. It was no longer just a place to kneel and recite familiar prayers; it was where he lingered, sometimes for hours, as though waiting for God Himself to descend and speak directly to his heart.

He lit a single candle that morning, watching the small flame flicker against the shadows of the sanctuary. The silence wrapped around him like a cloak, broken only by the faint creak of the wooden pew as he knelt.

His fingers laced tightly together, his lips moving in desperate whispers:

"Lord… make everything clear to me. I cannot carry this fog in my mind forever. If what I remember is true, if what I feel is real, then give me strength to face it. And if I am mistaken, erase these thoughts from me."

The memories haunted him—fragmented, blurred, yet insistent. He remembered the warmth of the wine, the heavy drowsiness that swept over him too suddenly to be natural, and the sensation of being half-awake yet unable to move. He remembered shadows bending over him, a weight pressing down, whispers he could not distinguish. Then blankness.

But when he woke up, he felt a deep understanding inside him. He knew that something had been taken. Something he could not name aloud.

He shook his head, clutching his chest as though he could keep his heart from breaking. "Was it real, Lord? Or am I deceiving myself?"

For so long, Mateo had been grateful to Fr. Alvarez. He had passed his final piano evaluation with flying colors—something he once thought impossible. The long hours of practice, the mentorship, the discipline… Alvarez had given him the tools to excel. Everyone congratulated him, but the triumph felt hollow now. What was success worth if his soul felt violated?

He bowed lower, forehead pressed against clasped hands. "I trusted him. I honored him as my guide. Why, then, do I feel this shame? Why this fear whenever I think of him?"

The crucifix above the altar seemed to gaze down at him, Christ's body stretched in silent suffering. Mateo felt both comforted and judged by those eyes.

Time passed—he did not know how long. The daylight shifted through the stained-glass windows, painting fragments of color across the floor. Seminarians came and went, kneeling briefly before moving on with their day. Mateo stayed. His body stiffened, his knees ached, but still he prayed.

Again and again, the same cry left his lips:

"Show me the truth, Lord. Even if it hurts. I cannot live in this darkness. Give me light, give me clarity."

Upon rising to leave, the weight of his burden left his legs unsteady. Yet a strange determination burned faintly within him. For the first time since that night, Mateo acknowledged to himself that the events with Alvarez were more than just a dream.

He did not yet know what to do with this knowledge. But he knew he could no longer run from it.

CHAPTER 32

The Quiet Distance

In the days that followed, Mateo's presence in the seminary shifted in ways so subtle that most did not notice. He still attended prayers, classes, and communal meals, still played the piano in the music room, and still offered a quiet smile when others greeted him. Yet beneath those familiar motions, something within him was breaking away.

He avoided being alone with Fr. Alvarez whenever possible. If the priest lingered after class, Mateo would excuse himself politely, saying he had extra chapel duties or lessons to review. If he was invited to dinner again, Mateo hesitated and fabricated a reason for not being able to attend. The old Mateo—eager, grateful, unquestioning—would never have refused.

But now a cautious watchfulness shadowed him.

At night, when the seminary was quiet and most of the brothers were asleep, Mateo returned to the chapel. The air smelled faintly of old wood and melted wax. He sat on the floor near the altar, his back against the pew, hands limp on his knees. Sometimes he prayed aloud, whispering every fragment of his confusion into the darkness. Other times, he said nothing at all—letting the silence itself be his prayer.

The memories remained fractured, but each time he turned them over in his mind, they seemed to fit together more clearly. The sudden heaviness in his body, the inability of his arms to obey him, and the shadow moving across his vision could not be mere imagination. It was too precise, too haunting. And the lingering sense of violation within him was something no dream could create.

"Why, Lord?" His voice cracked in the stillness. "Why would You let me trust someone who would harm me? Was the incident my fault? Did I invite such an act without knowing? Or… was I blinded because I wanted his approval too much?"

The crucifix above him gave no answer. Only the flame of the sanctuary lamp flickered steadily, a symbol of presence—mysterious, unchanging.

In the daylight, Mateo carried himself with dignity. He did not want to be seen as weak or to invite questions he was not ready to answer. Yet every time he glimpsed Fr. Alvarez—in the hallways, in the refectory, at Mass—a shiver crawled down his spine. He bowed respectfully, as he always had, but his eyes no longer lingered on the man he once admired.

He began journaling late at night, writing down prayers, questions, and half-formed thoughts he could not speak aloud. Page after page filled with words like *trust, betrayal, shame, silence,* and *truth.* Each word stared back at him like an open wound.

He was still unsure of his next step. Should he confide in another priest? Speak to the rector? Or would silence preserve him from being doubted, shamed, or accused of dishonoring a respected figure?

For now, Mateo chose the only refuge he could trust without question: the quiet stillness of God's presence.

And yet, beneath that stillness, a seed of resolve had begun to take root.

CHAPTER 33

The Burden of Silence

The thought came to Mateo late one evening as he lingered in the chapel: *Maybe I should tell someone.*

For days he had been carrying the weight of his fragmented memories, the gnawing ache in his soul, and the confusion that clouded his heart. He thought of Samuel, a fellow seminarian who had always been gentle and trustworthy, someone who once said to him, *"If ever you are burdened, Mateo, don't carry it alone."* Samuel was the kind of friend who would listen without judgement and not turn away.

The idea of speaking to him tugged at Mateo's heart. He even rehearsed it in his mind: how he might sit across from Samuel during their afternoon walk and how his voice would falter at first, then spill out the truth. He pictured Samuel's eyes widening in shock, then softening in compassion. Perhaps Samuel would urge him to go to the rector to make an official confession of what happened.

And then the image twisted. What if Samuel didn't believe him? What if he thought Mateo had misunderstood or, worse, had invited such closeness with Fr. Alvarez? The shame Mateo already felt threatened to drown him at the mere thought of suspicion. A priest's word carried authority; a seminarian's voice could be dismissed as confusion or, worse, rebellion.

The rector crossed Mateo's mind next. The old Monsignor was wise, respected, and had guided generations of seminarians toward the priesthood. Mateo wondered if the rector's calm gaze might pierce through the shadows that haunted him. But then, another fear surfaced: what if telling the rector meant scandal? What if, instead of help, it brought punishment, disgrace, or the shattering of his future?

Mateo's chest tightened as he knelt before the tabernacle, his forehead pressing against folded hands. Tears filled his eyes, blurring the golden glow of the sanctuary lamp.

"Lord," he whispered, "You know everything. You saw what I could not. You know the truth even if no one else ever does. I want to speak, but my tongue is chained by fear. If I tell them, what will become of me? What will become of this calling?"

His sobs were quiet, but they echoed in the emptiness of the chapel.

So he decided, for now, to keep everything to himself and God alone. He would bear the secret as a silent offering, trusting that God knew his heart even when he could not find the courage to explain it. His journal became the only place where he spoke fully—words poured out like wounds opened onto paper, then closed again when the cover snapped shut.

By day, he smiled and nodded, walked with the others, and bowed respectfully when he passed Fr. Alvarez. By night, he wrestled with the weight of silence until exhaustion finally took him.

It was not peace. But it was survival.

And survival, Mateo told himself, would have to be enough for now.

Chapter 34

A Whisper of Escape

The silence Mateo had chosen to keep was not gentle. It did not soothe him like the stillness of prayer or the quiet of the chapel at dawn. Instead, it was a heavy silence, one that pressed down on his chest and followed him like a shadow he could not shake.

Each day he moved through the seminary routines as if nothing were wrong: the morning prayers, the lectures on theology, the pastoral assignments, and the meals shared at long wooden tables. Outwardly he smiled, bowed respectfully to his professors, and even laughed faintly with his classmates when the moment demanded it. But inwardly, the silence gnawed at him.

He felt it most when he looked at Fr. Alvarez. The priest carried himself as though nothing had happened, offering Mateo the same guidance in music, scripture, and discipline as before. But to Mateo, each word, each look, was now tinged with an unbearable ambiguity. Was it genuine? Or was it another mask, another step in a deception Mateo still could not fully unravel?

At night, the silence became a torment. Mateo's mind replayed fragments of that evening—his drowsiness after the wine, the strange heaviness in his body, and the blurred impressions he could not fully remember. His soul screamed for clarity, yet his lips refused to speak. And so the silence grew heavier, weighing down even his prayers.

"Lord, am I still on Your path?" he whispered one evening. "Or have I been broken before I even began?"

Weeks later, the seminarians were sent on pastoral assignments to nearby communities: catechism classes, home visits, and assistance with local parish activities. Mateo welcomed the break, hoping the outside air might quiet the storm within him.

It was there, in the small coastal town where the sea breeze carried both salt and freedom, that he met Julian—a seminarian from another religious order, assigned to the same mission. Julian was a tall young man with a lightness about him, the kind of ease that made people open up without realizing it. He spoke with warmth, laughed easily, and carried no trace of the guarded stiffness that so many seminarians bore.

During one of their long walks back from visiting families, Julian asked casually, "How's the seminary life in your diocese? I hear each one has its own character."

Mateo hesitated, then forced a smile. "It's… disciplined. Demanding, but good for formation."

Julian chuckled. "Ours is strict, too, but the environment is different. The rector insists that we live like a family—transparent and supportive. If someone struggles, we don't carry it alone. It makes the burden lighter."

Mateo's chest tightened at the words. *Transparent. Supportive.* Those words felt completely unfamiliar to his experience. For a moment, he imagined himself in that environment, somewhere far from the weight of his silence, in a place where trust was possible again.

That night, lying in his temporary quarters, Mateo turned the thought over and over: *What if I left?*

The idea startled him, yet it also gave him a strange sense of hope. Moving to another seminary meant leaving behind the mentorship of Fr. Alvarez, the piano he had worked so hard to master, and the classmates who had become his brothers. But it also meant a chance to breathe freely, to step out of the shadows of confusion and fear, and to start anew.

Over the following weeks, the thought became a quiet resolution. He could no longer carry the silence where it was born. If he stayed, the weight would crush him. If he left, perhaps God would give him the space to heal.

One evening, back in the chapel of his seminary, Mateo knelt and whispered with trembling lips:

"Lord, if You still want me here, give me the courage to stay. If leaving is the only way to save my soul, then I will open the door and walk through it. I can't do this alone anymore."

The sanctuary lamp flickered, its flame steady and small, and Mateo felt within himself, for the first time in months, the faintest whisper of freedom.

He rose, his decision made. He would leave—not from the priesthood, not from the call he felt in his heart—but from this place that had wounded him. Somewhere far away, in a different seminary, he would begin again.

CHAPTER 35

The Weight of Departure

The decision to leave did not bring immediate peace.

At first, it felt like betrayal. Mateo found himself staring at the familiar walls of the seminary with an ache in his chest. These walls had been his home for years; he had laughed here, studied here, and prayed here. He had grown into himself under the watch of his brothers and mentors. To abandon it all felt like breaking a sacred vow, even if he knew none had yet been sealed.

Late at night, lying on his narrow bed, Mateo would clutch his rosary and whisper into the darkness:

"Am I running away, Lord? Or am I following You?"

Every word carried guilt. He thought of the rector, of the seminarians who trusted him, and of the parishioners who had encouraged him. What would they think if he left? Would they see him as weak, as a failure? Would whispers follow him for years, as though he had stained not just his own name but the honor of the seminary itself?

The fear was relentless. It wrapped around him during meals, when he forced himself to laugh at a friend's joke; it shadowed him in the lecture halls, when the professors spoke about sacrifice and endurance; it clung to him even in prayer, when silence became unbearable.

But alongside the fear, there was something else—something Mateo had not felt in months. Hope.

It came quietly, almost shyly, like a child knocking at the edge of his heart. When he remembered Julian's laughter, or the way the other seminarian had spoken of his seminary as a place of brotherhood rather than suspicion, Mateo felt a spark within him. Perhaps God was not asking him to abandon his vocation but to protect it—to preserve the flame by moving it to a place where it would not be smothered.

Still, the thought of leaving Fr. Alvarez tormented him. For years, this man had been his guide, shaping him not only in music but also in life. Mateo owed so much of his growth to him. And yet, behind that debt was the fracture of betrayal, the confusion of blurred memories, and the silence that poisoned Mateo's soul. *Could gratitude and hurt live in the same heart without destroying it?*

He found himself spending more hours than ever in the chapel. Sometimes he would kneel in silence, unable to form words, letting the ache speak for him. Other times, he prayed with intensity, whispering petitions like a man on the edge of drowning:

"Lord, I would rather not be lost. I don't want to lose Your calling. If leaving is against Your will, stop me. But if staying kills my soul, then forgive me for stepping away. Show me the way my heart can be whole again."

One night, as the chapel lay quiet in flickering candlelight, Mateo's strength finally gave way. He dropped to both knees before the crucifix and bowed low, forehead pressed to the cold marble floor. His rosary slipped from his fingers and scattered beads across the ground, but he did not move to gather them.

Tears broke free. He was not shedding restrained, silent tears; instead, he was sobbing, which wracked his chest and echoed faintly in the stillness of the sanctuary.

"I can't do this alone anymore," he whispered. His voice trembled, his throat raw. "I've carried it, Lord, and it's too heavy. I'm afraid of speaking. I'm afraid of staying. I'm afraid of leaving. I don't even know who I am anymore."

His palms pressed flat against the marble, as if he were clinging to something solid while his insides splintered apart.

"Take it," he cried. "Take the shame, the fear, the confusion—because it's crushing me. I don't know what's right anymore. But You do. So please, please, don't let me walk alone. If leaving is Your will, let me leave with peace. If staying is Your will, give me the strength not to drown."

The candles flickered as if stirred by an unseen breath. Mateo lifted his head slowly, eyes swollen, and fixed them on the crucifix. Christ's body, stretched and broken, seemed to gaze back at him—not with condemnation, but with a compassion Mateo had longed for in silence.

And in that gaze, something shifted. Not clarity, not certainty—but surrender. Mateo realized he did not need to carry the decision alone. He could place it in God's hands, trusting that even in his brokenness, he was not abandoned.

When at last he rose to his feet, his knees ached and his chest was sore from weeping, but his soul was lighter. The decision to leave still weighed on him, but now it no longer felt like his burden alone. It belonged to God.

And for the first time in months, Mateo felt he might actually sleep.

CHAPTER 36

Whispers of Confirmation

The morning after his tearful surrender in the chapel, Mateo woke with swollen eyes but a strange calm inside him. It wasn't peace, not fully, but it was gentler than the storm that had ruled his heart.

He went about the day as usual—morning prayers, lectures, meals with his friends—but everything felt slightly altered, as though the world had shifted by a degree overnight. He noticed details he had once overlooked: the warmth in a fellow seminarian's smile, the way sunlight spilled across the stained-glass windows, and the faint scent of incense lingering in the corridors. For the first time in months, he wasn't entirely trapped inside his own thoughts.

Still, doubts were whispered. *What if I'm just imagining all this? What if leaving is just an excuse to escape?* The guilt remained like a thorn in his side.

That week, Mateo was sent with another group of seminarians for pastoral work in the nearby community. He was paired again with Julian, the seminarian visiting from another seminary two provinces away. Their task was simple—visit homes, listen to stories, pray with the sick—but what struck Mateo most wasn't the work. Again, it was Julian himself.

Again, there was something light in the way Julian carried himself—someone free in his words. Over lunch, Julian spoke again about his seminary. He spoke not boastfully, nor as if he were comparing himself to others, but with the quiet ease of someone who didn't fear honesty.

"Our professors encourage us to ask questions," Julian said with a smile. "We're reminded that mistakes aren't shameful—they're part of the journey. And among the brothers, there's this sense… you can breathe. You don't have to hide your struggles."

Mateo listened intently, his heart tightening. He didn't speak of his own turmoil—he couldn't—but the way Julian described his seminary sounded like a different world. A place where light seeped in instead of shadows closing around him.

That night, back at the chapel, Mateo knelt before the tabernacle and whispered:

"Lord, is this what You're showing me? A place where I can still follow You… without suffocating?"

The candles flickered, and although silence lingered in response, something within his heart changed. He remembered Julian's words, the gentleness in his voice, and the absence of fear.

Over the following days, other signs appeared. A professor reminded the class, *"Vocation is not about where you begin—it is about where you are most able to hear God's voice."* A parishioner, in a passing conversation, told him, "God doesn't call you to a cage, hijo, but to freedom in His love." Even a homily at Mass carried weight when the priest spoke of Abraham leaving his homeland in faith, not knowing where God was leading him.

Piece by piece, these whispers began to weave a pattern Mateo could no longer ignore.

The decision was not yet acted upon, but within his heart, the balance was shifting. Fear lingered—fear of judgment, fear of failure, fear of losing everything—but beneath the fear was a quiet conviction forming like dawn breaking after a long night.

He did not know when or how, but he knew his path no longer lay here.

CHAPTER 37

A Door in the Mountains

By the end of his third year, the decision had quietly crystallized in Mateo's heart: he would leave the diocesan seminary.

The decision had not come suddenly or rashly but rather through a gradual accumulation of prayer, sleepless nights, and persistent whispers. Julian's passing words lingered in his memory, like a lamp left burning in a dark hallway. That brief encounter had shown Mateo that a different way existed—an image of formation not bound by fear and secrecy but open to truth and growth.

And so Mateo began to plan in silence. When his classmates rested, he sometimes slipped into the library, searching quietly for books and documents on seminaries across the country. Other times, he would linger after community work, asking discreet questions of priests and religious brothers about the paths one might take to transfer. It was not rebellion that guided him, but a yearning for life—life where he could serve God without suffocating.

Every night in prayer, he laid it before the Lord:

"If this is not Your will, close the door. If it is, show me the way."

As days turned into weeks, he felt overshadowed by fear, yet his conviction deepened.

It was during another pastoral work assignment that providence unfolded again. Mateo was paired with a seminarian named Arturo, a little older and studying under a different religious order. Arturo's demeanor was steady, with a calmness that drew people in. They spent the afternoon visiting families, praying with the elderly, and teaching catechism to children.

During a quiet walk back to the parish, Arturo began to speak—not of himself, but of the missionary spirit.

"You know, Mateo," he said thoughtfully, "there's more than one path to priesthood. Not all of us are meant to stay in the diocesan way. Some are called to be missionaries, to go where the Church is most in need—mountains, islands, places the world forgets."

Mateo's steps slowed. He glanced at Arturo, unsure if the words were casual or intentional. "Missionaries?" he asked softly.

Arturo nodded. "Yes. I belong to a religious order called the Missionaries of the Word. Our formation house is far from here, on another island, in the mountains. It's not easy—life there is simpler and harder—but it's full of meaning. We are trained to serve in distant lands, sometimes in foreign countries, always with people who hunger for God in places others rarely reach."

The words struck Mateo's heart with force. Mountains. Another island. A different way. He felt as though Arturo had unknowingly put into words the very longing he had been carrying.

That night in the chapel, Mateo could not keep still. He sat, stood, and knelt again, pacing like a restless soul before God's presence.

"Lord, is this it? Is this why You've been stirring my heart? Am I called not just to leave, but to go—to be sent, to carry You where few dare to go?"

The silence pressed around him, yet it was not empty. It was the silence of waiting, of God listening, of God shaping. And Mateo, though still trembling with fear, felt something rise within him—a daring hope that his calling might be wider than the walls of the seminary he knew.

The pieces were falling into place. Julian's spark, Arturo's words, his own restless prayers—woven together like threads in a tapestry he could only glimpse from the underside. He did not yet know how the pattern would unfold, but for the first time in a long time, he felt the stirrings of freedom, and with it, the courage to take his first steps into the unknown.

CHAPTER 38

The Visitor in the Lobby

The afternoon was quiet, the kind of quiet Mateo cherished. He carried with him a few folded notes he had been scribbling from his research—details about the Missionaries of the Word, their formation process, and their missionary work across the world. His plan was simple: slip into the library, read in silence, pray for clarity, and keep moving toward the life he had already begun to imagine.

But the speakers cracked to life, their metallic echo spreading across the seminary halls:

"Mateo, you have a visitor in the lobby."

He froze mid-step. The papers nearly slipped from his hand. A visitor? For him? He rarely received any.

His family lived far, and few outsiders ever sought him personally.

Then the porter repeated it:

"Mateo, a visitor is waiting for you in the lobby."

His chest tightened. The corridor stretched before him like a tunnel, his ears filled with the pounding of his own heartbeat.

When he finally summoned the courage to ask a passing seminarian who it was, the words dropped like stones into his stomach.

"It's a woman named… Miss Lolita."

Time slowed. The name alone was enough to drag Mateo back into San Agustin—the place he had tried so hard to bury in silence. He was haunted by blurred memories, shadows, and shame. His body remembered what his mind had tried to suppress.

He stood frozen, his legs refusing to move toward the lobby. Every instinct told him to run in the opposite direction, to disappear into the library, and to beg the porter to say he was unavailable. But the announcement had already rung through the seminary walls. His name had been called twice. Everyone knew a visitor had come specifically for him. To refuse to appear would stir questions, whispers, and suspicions.

Swallowing hard, Mateo forced himself down the stairs, each step heavier than the last.

The lobby felt unbearably open, exposed. And there she was.

Miss Lolita stood with an expression caught between feigned casualness and quiet insistence. She had told the porter she was visiting someone else, but her eyes searched only for him the moment he entered.

"Mateo," she said softly, almost too gently for the space.

He felt the sting of betrayal all over again, though she had done nothing in that moment but speak his name. His body betrayed him too—his palms sweated, his throat constricted, and his legs trembled as if he were still the frightened boy from San Agustin.

He wanted to say something sharp, something final, but no words came. Instead, silence pressed between them.

Miss Lolita clasped her hands, lowering her voice so the seminarians passing through would not overhear. "I only wanted to see how you are… It has been long, and I thought perhaps—"

Mateo cut her off, his voice shaking. "Why are you here? You should not have come."

She flinched at the coldness in his tone but did not step back. "I—I was in the area. I wanted to make sure you were all right. That's all."

All right. The words pierced him. Did she know the weight her presence carried? Did she know she was summoning ghosts he had been battling night after night in prayer?

"Please," he whispered, his eyes darting toward the others moving about the lobby. "Leave. Don't come here again."

Miss Lolita's lips parted, perhaps to defend herself, perhaps to plead, but something in Mateo's gaze—desperate, resolute—made her hesitate. For a moment, she lingered as though she might refuse. But finally, she turned and left with a nod so small that it could have been mistaken for a bow.

Mateo stood rooted in place long after the door shut behind her. His chest heaved with shallow breaths. He wanted to collapse, to scream, to confess to someone the torrent of memories clawing at him. Instead, he clenched his notes tighter, retreating inward.

He returned to the chapel before the library. He fell to his knees, pressing his forehead to the pew.

"Lord, why now? Why her? Why here? I thought I was moving forward. Why do You let the past chase me like this?"

The silence of the chapel gave no answer, but his tears finally came, streaming down unchecked. The unexpected burden of her visit made his resolve both weaker and stronger: weaker, for it reminded him of his wounds; stronger, for it made him certain that he could not heal here, not in this seminary where shadows still stalked him.

He needed distance. He needed a new beginning. He needed the mountains.

Mateo walked out of the chapel with red eyes, but his heart was no longer wavering. Miss Lolita's sudden appearance had torn open wounds he thought were healing, but instead of weakening him, the encounter clarified everything. He could not remain here, in a place that carried the same air as San Agustin—the same silence that covered secrets, the same corridors where betrayal could walk freely, the same walls where trust had once been shattered.

Her visit was not a simple intrusion; it was a revelation. The past would always find him here. The ghosts would never stop knocking at these doors. If he stayed, he would always be one step away from collapse, from breaking under the weight of memories that others insisted on pretending never happened.

He needed distance—not just from her, but from all of it. He needed distance from the manipulation that was disguised as mentorship, the smiles that concealed cruelty, and the voices that demanded obedience while breaking his spirit. He had offered his heart in trust, and in return, they pierced it with arrows sharpened by betrayal.

No more.

Miss Lolita's presence had sealed it. Mateo now knew, with a clarity deeper than any library research or whispered advice could offer: he needed to leave, to cross the sea, to climb into the mountains where the Missionaries of the Word formed its seminarians. Only there, far away from these ruins of faith and trust, could he begin again.

This decision was not born of escape alone, but of survival, of dignity, of the stubborn belief that God had not abandoned him—even if people had. And in that painful certainty, Mateo felt a strange, quiet strength.

For the first time, leaving was not just an idea. It was his path.

CHAPTER 39

The Final Turning Point

As the school year ended, Mateo's heart carried both the weight of farewell and the quiet fire of hope. The confirmations had all been finalized: his transfer was approved, and his request accepted. The path ahead no longer seemed hidden in shadow but illuminated, as if each step was already prepared for him long before he found the courage to walk it.

He left the diocesan seminary without ceremony. There was no dramatic goodbye, no explanation to those who might wonder why he was choosing a different road. He carried only his belongings and the invisible scars of the years spent within those walls. What he did not carry—what he refused to carry—was the bitterness of betrayal. He had resolved to place that in God's hands, to let the new chapter of his life become the ground for healing rather than another prison of memory.

The Missionaries of the Word welcomed him first as a postulant. For one month, Mateo immersed himself in the rhythm of community life, silence, prayer, and the quiet joy of beginning anew. Unlike the heaviness that had marked his former days, here the air felt lighter, freer. The formators spoke not only of obedience and discipline, but also of mission, of walking with the poor, of carrying the Gospel to the edges of the world. Mateo found in those words the faint echo of the call he had heard long ago—the one that had led him into the seminary in the first place, before all the shadows came.

However, the relocation to the Missionaries of the Word seminary in the Santa Monica mountains solidified his decision. The novitiate was perched high in the mountains of another island, a place where the fog embraced the trees at dawn and the evenings ended with the sound of cicadas rising from the forest. The journey itself was long and arduous, crossing seas and winding roads, but Mateo felt no fatigue. Every mile placed between him and San Agustin was a release, as though God Himself was untying the cords of his past.

When he finally arrived at Sta. Monica, he paused at the entrance gate, his breath caught by the sight before him. The seminary was simple but modern, yet it radiated an atmosphere of quiet majesty. Wooden buildings with red-tiled roofs blended seamlessly with the surrounding mountainside. Terraced gardens overflowed with vegetables and flowers, tended by novices during their work periods. At the very heart of the compound stood the main chapel, its bell tower rising humbly yet firmly toward the sky.

The chapel became Mateo's refuge almost instantly. Inside, the air was cool, scented faintly with burning candles and polished wood. There was no grandeur, no imposing architecture like in San Agustin—only simplicity. But in that simplicity, Mateo felt God more present than he had in years. The crucifix above the altar seemed to look at him not with judgment but with compassion, as if Christ Himself was whispering, "You *are home now.*"

Daily life in Sta. Monica unfolded with a rhythm that nourished him. Dawn began with the ringing of the chapel bell, calling the novices to morning prayer. After the Liturgy of the Hours, they ate breakfast together in silence, followed by classes on theology, scripture, and missionary spirituality. Afternoons were given to manual labor—tending the gardens, repairing fences, and cooking meals. Evenings closed again in prayer, their voices rising in hymn as the sun sank behind the mountains, painting the sky in gold and violet.

The silence of the mountains became his greatest teacher. No longer did he hear the echoes of betrayal; instead, he heard birdsong, the rustle of leaves, and the rhythm of his own breathing as he walked the paths between chapel and dormitory. Each sound reminded him that life was continuing, that creation itself was testifying to a God who makes all things new.

Here, Mateo's wounds did not vanish—but they began to heal. Slowly. Quietly.

And though the memories of San Agustin and the old seminary walls would never vanish completely, Mateo no longer feared them. They had led him here, to this mountain, to this life. They had carved in him the space where God's grace could finally take root.

For the first time in years, Mateo felt at peace.

Chapter 40
A New Beginning

The first month at Sta. Monica was unlike anything Mateo had ever experienced in his years of formation. Life here was not centered on rigid rules or cold hierarchies, but on the living Word of God. Every day began with Scripture. The novices were taught to hold the Bible not as a book of obligation but as a lamp for the journey, a companion to wrestle with and be guided by.

"Let the Word shape you; let it breathe in you," their novice master reminded them often. And Mateo, still carrying wounds of betrayal and mistrust, found in the Psalms the language of his soul: his cries, his laments, and his quiet songs of hope. For the first time in years, Scripture was no longer an academic text to be dissected but a living voice that spoke directly into his silence.

Alongside their studies and daily rhythm of prayer, the novices were led into spiritual exercises meant to ground them in their vocation. Among these was the Marian retreat—a ten-day spiritual experience set aside to honor Mary, the Mother of Jesus. Though it was meant as an introduction to Marian devotion for the first-year novices, it would become, for Mateo, a doorway into an experience that would mark him forever.

One evening, after hours of guided prayer and reflection, Mateo went to bed weary but at peace. Yet sometime in the night, he dreamt—or perhaps it was more than a dream—that he was being led gently down the narrow road that wound toward the gates of the seminary. There, just as the road curved, stood the grotto of the Blessed Virgin Mary: a small cave with her statue, hands folded in prayer, her gaze tender and unwavering.

In his dream, Mateo did not hear words, but he felt them—like a mother's embrace, firm yet consoling. Mary's presence seemed to speak directly to his heart as the Lady in the Grotto: *"Do not be afraid, my son. I am with you. What you have lost, God will restore. What was broken, He will make whole."*

He awoke with tears on his face, unsure if he had dreamed or truly been led. Yet when he walked past the grotto the next morning on his way to the chapel, the memory of the night returned with such clarity that he felt he was standing once more before the statue of the Blessed Virgin Mary. From that day forward, Mateo knew he could entrust his wounds, his fears, and his calling to her care.

During this 10-day silent retreat—a profound initiation into the novitiate—this devotion blossomed. Surrounded by silence, prayer, and Scripture, Mateo discovered a new dimension of his faith. In moments of struggle, he returned in prayer to the image of Mary, the Lady at the Grotto, holding him in her gaze. It was no longer just a statue at the seminary entrance but a living reminder of God's tenderness made visible in the Mother of Christ.

For the first time, Mateo experienced what true devotion meant—not superstition, not ritual obligation, but a relationship: a heart drawn into the maternal love of Mary, who always points the way back to her Son.

By the end of those ten days, something within him had shifted. The bitterness of San Agustin had loosened its grip. The shadows of betrayal no longer haunted every corner of his mind. His vocation no longer felt like an escape from pain but a response to love—a love that had pursued him even through darkness, a love that had brought him here, to the mountains of Sta. Monica.

Standing once again before the grotto after the retreat, Mateo whispered with a steadiness he had not known in years:

"Here I am, Lord. Heal me. Send me. Make me Yours."

And with that, his new beginning truly began.

Epilogue

Looking back, a long series of wounds and trials had shaped Mateo's life. From his earliest years, the shadows of suffering followed him. His childhood was scarred by ordeals that stripped away innocence too soon. What once was a home filled with warmth and parental love shifted, over time, into a household of rules, stern correction, and cold distance. His parents, who had once embraced him with gentleness, became stricter, harder, and more demanding—perhaps in their own fears, perhaps in their unspoken disappointments.

The failures of his siblings in their own pursuits only deepened this change. Each downfall left heavy expectations placed on Mateo's shoulders, as though he were the last hope to restore the family's honor. And into this fragile landscape stepped Miss Lolita—whose manipulation, masked as affection, left scars far deeper than anyone could see. Her abuse and betrayal pierced Mateo's trust in ways that would haunt him through his youth.

It was this torment, this hunger to escape, that led Mateo first into the diocesan seminary. He sought refuge within its walls, where the discipline and order gave him a sense of belonging and purpose. There, the tolling of the bell became the rhythm of his existence. The bell was constant, unrelenting, commanding every moment of his day. It called him to prayer, to study, to work, and to silence. Though at first it felt oppressive, over time the bell became something more: a reminder that beyond human cruelty and frailty, there was still a Voice calling him to rise, to endure, to follow.

Yet, even within the seminary's walls, betrayal found him once again. Fr. Alvarez, whose words promised guidance and whose presence should have embodied fatherhood and care, deceived and manipulated instead. The very place where Mateo had sought safety became another field of wounds. But unlike before, Mateo's spirit did not collapse. Instead, this deception became a breaking point that forged a new resolve.

The bell, once a symbol of control, had become a teacher. Its unyielding summons revealed to him that his true calling was not confined by San Agustin's walls nor bound to the ambitions of men who sought power rather than service. His vocation was not born of fear, nor of escape, but of love—love shaped in suffering, yet yearning to be free.

And so, Mateo made his choice. With a steady heart, he walked away from San Agustin, leaving behind betrayal and manipulation, and set his path toward the mountains of Sta. Monica. There, in the quiet and simplicity of the Missionaries of the Word, he found a new beginning. The rugged road to the novitiate was not just a physical journey but a spiritual one: a path away from the wounds of his past and into the embrace of healing, purpose, and hope.

The child who once sought refuge had become the man who now sought a mission. The bell that once dictated his life now echoed within him—not as an oppressor, but as a call to live faithfully, courageously, and freely.

And in the silence of the mountains, standing before the grotto of the Blessed Virgin Mary, Mateo understood at last: what had been broken was not the end of his story. It was the beginning of the man God was calling him to become.

(To be continued in "They Can See You")